THE ALTERING MACHINE

ERIKA HARKEN

THE ALTERING MACHINE

Cover Designer: Erika Harken
www.erikaharken.com

ISBN-13: 978-1-7376640-7-9
Library of Congress Control Number: 2023922661

First Edition: February 2024
Printed in the United States of America

VERUM FICTA PRESS
An imprint of Isaiah Publishing Co.

Davison, Michigan.

Contents

THE
ALTERING
MACHINE

DARK ORIGIN

BECKY

1 - PREY

Becky Johnson peeked at the front doors of the library through a line of books while sliding a few geographical volumes into place. It was almost six thirty that evening—the time Paul Henderson normally came to the local library in Carson City after his work shift across town.

Becky wore a small smile at the thought of her last encounter with him the day before, when they had talked for nearly forty-five minutes. Aside from Paul explaining the fascinating experiments he performed at the research lab, they had also talked about more personal things—like their favorite mountain trails, the last movie they saw, and what each of them were up to that weekend.

I'm glad last Saturday was busier than normal so I didn't sound pathetic saying I had nothing going on this weekend, but... does he want to hang out?

She pushed her chunky bangs out of her eyes and sighed, then walked toward the bathroom in a nearby hallway. Inside it, the yellow ceiling lights glowed dimly above the three stalls and sinks, and Becky stared at herself in the mirror, studying her appearance for any necessary adjustments before Paul saw her.

Becky wore a white blouse under a gray fleece jacket, along with a knee-length black skirt, sheer tights, and formal black flats. The outfit was among a large, similar collection of pieces that fit her image of a professional librarian—even if the clothes seemed to age her several years beyond twenty-three.

Paul knows I don't dress like this outside of work, right? I want to look knowledgeable and serious here, but he's so smart, I'm sure he thinks I have better style than this...

Becky swept her shoulder-length black hair into a ponytail and turned her head, wondering if her locks looked best up or down. Her eyebrows were thin above her thick lashes, and her large nose and small mouth rested within a pale, clear complexion.

Would Paul like my hair up? Kind of impossible to tell...

Becky sighed Sand turned from the mirror, leaving the bathroom in annoyance. She walked to the west end of the library where shelves of books on all scientific topics and theories were—but it was also the place Paul would go once he arrived, and Becky slipped behind a desk to busy herself with computer work. But while she killed time, the anticipation caused her cheeks to grow warm and created a tickling sensation in her stomach. After twenty minutes, the sound of heavy footsteps made Becky peer up from the staff computer.

Her blood raced as she watched Paul walk toward her wearing a thin, red flannel jacket, navy scrubs, and black boots. His dirty blond hair hung in front of his brown eyes, and the fluorescent ceiling lights reflected glaringly off the large lenses of his glasses.

Becky stopped typing while she stared, and soon, Paul stood in front of her.

"Hey Becky," Paul said, his husky voice low.

"Hi Paul," she replied happily. "How was your shift today?"

"Excellent," he replied, his eyes widening. "There were a few new breakthroughs in my radiation experiments."

"Excellent," Becky repeated. "I'm sorry, but there are a ton of internet checkouts and I don't have a lot of time to talk tonight. But if you still don't have plans this weekend, I..."

She failed to finish as her heart pounded loudly in her ears, and a small smile turned the corner of Paul's mouth as he stared at her.

"Do you want to see me this Saturday?" he asked.

"Yes—um—yes."

"I would love to see you, too, Becky. What's your number?"

Becky grinned as she reached for a pen, then jotted her number down on the corner of a yellow legal pad. After tearing it off, she handed the piece of paper to him.

"Text or call me—whatever works," she blurted, her cheeks flushing.

I'm so shameless...

Paul pinched the paper between his thumb and index finger, brushing his skin against the tips of Becky's fingers. She bit her lip at their first touch, her gaze falling away while the small smile on Paul's lips remained.

● ● ● ● ● ●

The darkening sky had a striking orange edge above the trees across the road while Becky waited for Paul to pick her up that Saturday evening. She stood beside her bedroom window with her cell phone in hand, his last text message telling her he would arrive soon.

Becky chose one of her favorite, more *lively* outfits to wear that night—a purple crop top, high waist shorts with a few rips, and a black belt, along with her gray zip-up jacket. A silver chain with a heart locket also hugged her neck, and her ankle-high black boots had a thick, two-inch heel.

Becky stared at the dark road at the end of the driveway as if she were unable to look away, but her fixation was eventually rewarded by the headlights of Paul's decades-old, rusted truck turning toward the house. Becky turned instantly and left her messy room behind, dashing into the upstairs hallway and down the staircase. She shouted goodbye to her parents before the front door slammed behind her and quickly made her away toward Paul's red and white truck.

Becky jerked the passenger door open and climbed into the empty seat beside him, shyly saying *hello* as she fastened her seat belt. Paul smiled at her in the dark cabin of the old pickup.

"You look very nice, Becky," he said, his voice husky and calm.

"So do you," she replied. "I like your hair combed."

Her eyes fell from the right-side part in his gelled hair to his clothes, which were also different that night. Paul wore a button-up black dress shirt beneath his usual red flannel jacket, and his dark wash jeans looked clean and new. Both of them sat quietly as Paul backed out of the driveway onto the main road, and Becky began to fidget with her heart locket.

"You're lying about not going to this drive-in before."

Becky blinked and looked at him, uncertain by his even tone if he was joking.

"I'm not lying, I promise," she insisted. "I've never met someone who wanted to go and they're rare these days—"

"Relax," Paul said with a small smile. "I wasn't serious."

"Oh!" Becky replied with a laugh. "I—I should have known. How many times have you been to the drive-in?"

"I go all the time, but tonight is special, Becky. I can't wait for you to see *Hollow Suburbia*... my favorite."

She smiled at him and thought about the plot of the movie again, which he had described to her through a few text messages earlier. *Hollow Suburbia* told the story of a woman who traded her real life for a simulation, though the switch ultimately had fatal consequences.

"When did that movie come out?" she asked. "I don't think I've ever heard of it."

"More than twenty years ago, but it's an independent film, so I doubt anyone has heard much about it. The drive-in plays it twice a month, though, and that's how I first saw it."

A comfortable silence settled between them, and Becky stared at the dirt road while it disappeared beneath the truck, trying to imagine her own life existing perfectly inside a simulated environment. Although the idea seemed appealing, she wondered how perfect perfection could really be.

"What if you could live in a perfect world, Becky? Every last little thing the way you wanted it?"

Her eyes widened as she tried to hide her surprise, for it felt as though Paul had read her mind. Becky shrugged slightly and put a hand on the side of her neck.

"The thought is tempting, that's for sure. There's a lot I would change about the world and my life."

"Yes… it's only natural. But in your perfect world… how would you look?"

Becky furrowed her eyebrows and looked at him. Paul sat motionless beside her, his gaze heavily cast through the windshield.

"What do you mean exactly?"

"Well… would you give yourself a new body?"

A brief silence fell between them as Becky considered the idea seriously.

"Sure—why not?" she replied. "I used to want to look like a magazine model, but it's not realistic for me, or a lot of people. But inside a simulation, of course."

As Becky watched him, a wide, sealed-lip smile spread across Paul's face.

"You're right, Becky. It's not realistic for a lot of people to look very beautiful, or have happy lives. But those with extreme beauty have an advantage over the rest of us. Anything they want in life will come easier because of how they look—jobs, relationships, friends, money, praise—anything. Beauty is worth seeking and obtaining by any means, and the radiation experiments I've told you about… they're all for the sake of it."

Becky raised a brow, trying to rationalize his confident reasoning as she bit her lip.

"You're using radiation to… create beauty?"

"Yes. Radiation can mutate the DNA of a living thing and create all kinds of effects and possibilities. But I've been experimenting with a particular kind of radiation that has successfully altered the appearance of my test subjects without any negative effects, and it's led to great enhancements."

Becky's blood raced as she imagined a human trapped inside a metal chamber while having their genes manipulated with endless amounts of radiation.

"Test subjects? What kind?"

"Rabbits."

She sighed and managed to relax, but only a little. Despite the eeriness that still hung in the air, Becky's morbid curiosity won over.

"What did you do to them?" she asked quietly.

"You can see for yourself very soon. But they're no longer prey, Becky."

2 - HELP

A week later, Paul sat in a pale green booth at the back of a small, brightly lit diner around seven o'clock. He stared down at the white mug of coffee in his hand, his thoughts fixated on the *machine*—which he had taken apart and rebuilt over the last few days in his basement.

The rabbits had also left the research lab and lived in a cage near the machine, but his experiments on them—though quite successful—were losing satisfaction.

I need more than small animals... I need the type of subject the machine was created for to exercise its true power. But how do I get a human?

Paul lifted the coffee mug to his lips and sipped, his mind shifting to Becky. He expected her to enter the diner at any moment, and despite a brief effort not to picture her in his machine, the idea grew exciting, and soon overwhelmed him.

She just needs a few DNA alterations... simple improvements to her face and legs. But she could be Sadie, she could be absolutely perfect if I took my time...

Paul continued to sip his coffee while his mind entertained endless possibilities of what Becky could become. When the bell above the diner door softly jingled, he glanced across the restaurant and saw Becky walk in, her expression brightening as their eyes met. She made her way past a line of empty booths and slid into the seat across from him, her cheeks already flushed.

"Hi Paul," she said cheerfully. "How was your day?"

"Good, but you've made it much better. Yours?"

"I helped an old lady find a book she loved as a kid without knowing the title or author," Becky replied proudly. "I can't tell you how many keyword searches I did to help her find it, but after some close matches and shelf digging, we finally found it! I've been warm and fuzzy ever since."

Paul's smile widened as joy beamed from Becky's face. He also felt a similar warmth when he was with her, and for a moment, it seemed she had the perfect beauty he longed for since childhood.

"You're incredible, Becky... so helpful and kind," he said, his quiet tone in awe. "You're perfect, almost."

Becky laughed a little and rolled her eyes.

"I'm far from perfect. Did you order?"

"No."

Becky reached for a menu and Paul studied her while she read it, uncertain if he wanted Becky inside his machine or not. Although another woman had never compared to Sadie's natural beauty, he found he still enjoyed gazing at Becky, and that she could be quite pretty in her own, unique way. But the conflict inside him paused when a waitress appeared at their table, taking their double order of a cheeseburger and fries. After she left, Becky looked at him again with a smile.

"How hard was it to move and rebuild the machine?" she asked curiously. "I can't imagine how busy that kept you all week."

"Certainly not easy," Paul replied. "But I know it like the back of my hand. The machine is fully operational now after spending many long, late nights on it."

"I can't believe the company let you take it. Doesn't it belong to them?"

"It did, but the machine has no practical or legal use for them, so I bought it. The machine is very powerful, Becky... it's capable of so much. But only I truly know what it can do—no one has put more work into its creation than me."

Becky's mystified eyes poured into his, raising the hair across his skin in excitement. Clearly the machine intrigued her, and he wanted her near or inside it as soon as possible.

"Becky, you should come for dinner at my house tomorrow night," he said eagerly. "I will cook for you, and then you can see it—the *machine*—and my very special rabbits."

She nodded once and smiled, snapping out of her slight trance.

"Where do you live?"

"In the mountains outside of town, between here and Genoa. It's the house I grew up in and inherited after my parent's death."

Becky's brow furrowed as the corners of her mouth turned down.

"Your parents are dead?"

"Yes. My mother died when I was twelve, and my dad passed away several years ago. But I also inherited a lot of money... which has been very useful."

"Oh... is that how you bought the DNA-altering machine?"

"Yes, and how I paid for my degree."

"Your degree is in biochemistry, right?" Becky asked. "Where did you go?"

Paul's grip tightened around his white coffee mug while a sudden strike of anger coursed through him. It was rare that he spoke or thought of his college days anymore, except for the best part of it all—*Sadie*.

"Strathsmith University," he said at length, his tone even.

"Wow—really? That place is so beautiful and prestigious! I bet it was amazing to go there."

Paul took a deep breath as he forced his hand to loosen around the coffee mug. A few of his darkest memories began on the grounds of that campus, and though he wouldn't share the whole truth with her, Paul craved Becky's sympathy, for he had been horribly wronged.

* * * * * *

EIGHT YEARS EARLIER

Paul walked alone to his freshman biology class early one Monday morning. While he made his way to the largest science building, he passed a few other students who also seemed to have slept well and were not invited to any parties that weekend—not that it terribly bothered him.

He entered a large metal door and walked down a long white hallway to his classroom that sat in the middle of the building. And just as expected, no one else had arrived twenty minutes early—not even the professor. Paul enjoyed a dose of pride as he took his usual seat at a table in the back of the room, opening his messenger bag to pull out a textbook and notebook.

To pass the time, he started reading the homework chapter again, though his mind gradually drifted to another classmate, and when *she* might walk through the door. Her slim figure, glossy black hair, delicate facial features and deep brown eyes had fueled his obsessive attraction since class began months ago, and Paul couldn't wait to lay eyes on her again.

Sadie... she's perfect.

His gaze settled on her chair at the front of the room, imagining himself brave enough to walk up and talk to her... or even show up at a campus party. But as much as he enjoyed fantasies of her, the beauty of Sadie's form faded into the haunting memory of his mother crying inconsolably at her vanity many years ago. She didn't know that he watched her from the slight gap of the bedroom door, and at the age of twelve, he couldn't understand why her face had ended her dreams.

Paul's throat tightened while he sank into more tragic memories of her—until a few loud classmates burst through the door and shocked him back to reality. Paul shifted uncomfortably in his seat and stared at his textbook as the classroom began to fill and the professor arrived. He didn't look for Sadie as he tried to ignore the pain coursing through him, but the slow poison of her presence soon became his antidote. The seat next to him—which normally stayed empty—was suddenly occupied.

Sadie met his gaze and smiled perfectly at him, causing his pain to quickly evaporate. Paul watched hungrily as she pulled her things from her backpack, admiring every part of her all over again. Because of her perfection, he knew the advantage she possessed in life, but his craving told him to possess her.

"Hi. You're Peter, right? I'm Sadie."

Paul blinked and nodded once, not caring that she had mistaken his name.

"Do you think you could help me study for the exam?" Sadie asked, her tone concerned. "I've noticed you're the smartest person in class, and all this biology stuff doesn't make sense to me."

As her helpless gaze peered into his, Paul felt hypnotized into agreement, though he would have helped willingly even if she demanded it.

"Yes," he replied eagerly. "When, Sadie... when would..."

"Are you busy tonight?"

Paul shook his head quickly.

"Great—my dorm is in the Ruefort Hall building. Can you stop by at seven?"

"Of course."

"Thanks. Do you mind if I take a peek at your homework?" she asked innocently. "I fell asleep last night when I was trying to do it and missed a few answers."

Paul pulled the homework sheet from the front of his notebook and passed it to her. While Sadie quickly copied the answers before class began, he smiled a little and reflected on watching her through her dorm window the night before. She hadn't touched any homework but spent the evening with her boyfriend, who stayed past the time Paul decided to return to his own dorm.

He didn't mind her little lies.

3 - THEORY

Paul sat at the desk in Sadie's dorm room correcting her homework mistakes like he had done several times in the last few weeks. And while he kept busy, Sadie carefully painted her toenails on the floor across the room as music played. Although few words were said during their homework sessions, Paul still felt satisfied to be alone with her—to observe Sadie closely without hiding and memorize her personal belongings.

On the shelf above her bed, a few personal items were on display: a framed picture of her and another young woman at a concert; an old, half-empty perfume bottle; a standing condolence card and a small jewelry box.

Paul imagined taking any one of them back to his own dorm to study and treasure, were it not for how easily Sadie would notice the item missing. But if he could take one, he would have to touch her bed sheets, which always looked fresh and soft...

"How bad is it?"

Paul blinked, his thoughts broken.

"What, Sadie?"

"My homework. How horrible is it?"

"Did you read the chapter?"

Sadie smiled and laughed a little.

"Not all of it. It's really hard for anything in this class to stick."

"I understand. Don't worry—I'm fixing it."

He watched as her lips spread into a wide, perfectly beautiful smile. Paul's gaze swept down the rest of her body covered by a tight pink tank top and gray running shorts. Sadie's long black hair tumbled in waves around her shoulders, and even without makeup, no other woman he had ever seen could compare.

Paul turned away from her with difficulty, struggling to clear his mind of her tantalization as he prepared to finish her homework.

"What was your last date like?"

Her soft voice flowed warmly into him, preventing any hope of escape.

"We went to a museum."

Sadie grinned, giggling.

"How long ago was that?"

"High school."

"What grade?"

"Sophomore year."

"Oh—it's been a while. Did you comb your hair or get dressed up?"

"No, Sadie."

She rose from the floor and motioned to him, her other hand on her hip. Paul raised a brow and slowly stood, then took a few long strides toward her. When Sadie took a step back to make more space between them, he didn't feel embarrassed.

"I know you need these," she remarked, her fingertips falling lightly on either side of his glasses. "But they're not very modern, or cute. You should try contacts if you want another date soon."

Sadie pulled the old, thick glasses from his face, tossing them on top of her bed. Paul's gaze flashed to her sheets, which he now had an excuse to touch.

"Those were my father's."

Sadie didn't respond as she swept his long bangs to one side, her gaze narrowing as she studied the red blemishes across his complexion.

"Most girls like guys with short hair, but if you want to keep it long, part it to one side and shape it with some gel. You should also start a skincare routine—there are plenty of acne products out there."

Paul nodded, his gaze sinking deep into hers as he relished the nearness of her heavenly form. Sadie smiled uncomfortably and looked away, turning toward the bookshelf behind her. There, she grabbed a small yellow tube with a red cap and pressed it against his chest moments later.

"This is the best chapstick I've ever used," she said. "I'm sure you know how important hydration is, but this will also help with your cracked lips."

Paul said nothing and raised his hand, laying it gently on top of hers. The softness of it made his pulse quicken while he savored their innocent touch, and Sadie reluctantly met his gaze.

"This chapstick has been on your lips, Sadie?"

"Yes... of course," she replied, uneasy.

Paul smiled slightly as his eyes focused on her full lips, which had the perfect, natural shade of red. Unlike his face, Sadie's creamy complexion bore no imperfections, and he entertained the thought of stroking her cheek, and bringing her lips closer.

"Sadie... you're..."

Incredible heat rose across his body as his desire for her intensified, becoming almost uncontrollable. Paul's hand tightened around hers suddenly, his hunger feeling impossible to restrain the longer they stood so close and alone. Although satisfaction would start with a kiss, Paul craved much more, and as he prepared himself, the door to her room swung open.

Sadie gasped and tore her hand away, her attention focused on another young man standing in the doorway. His gelled hair and handsome face equaled her beauty, and he wore blue jeans, a black t-shirt, and a varsity jacket.

"Jordan!" Sadie said, relieved. "What are you doing here? I thought you went to a game with Michael."

"It was canceled right after we got there," he replied, his tone annoyed. "What's going on here?"

Paul studied Jordan quickly, noticing his taller height and obvious muscular build. Sadie left him to stand at Jordan's side, her hands grasping his arm.

"Just a little study session for biology. Jordan, this is—"

"Paul, right?"

Paul nodded once, his gaze shifting from Jordan's. He knew Sadie's boyfriend recognized him from the same place he did—their Thursday afternoon economics class. And though they had never spoken, Paul heard his name mentioned a few times among Jordan and his friends while they sat behind him and made fun of him.

"Are you almost done here?" Jordan asked. "I want to go downtown tonight."

"We're definitely done," Sadie replied. "Thanks for everything, Paul. You're the *best*."

Paul glanced at her, his hunger still alive as he retrieved his glasses from her bed. After grabbing his textbook and messenger bag, he kept his gaze on the floor as he walked past them into the hall. But after a short distance, he stopped when he heard Jordan's voice.

"Don't study with him anymore, Sadie. He's weird and I don't trust him."

Paul's shoulders tensed, his anger simmering as he frowned.

"I know he's weird and kind of unsettling..." she replied. "But I can't pass Biology without him. What do you expect me to do?"

"How about getting a real tutor through the learning center?"

"No, Jordan. A *real* tutor isn't going to fill in the answers for me while I get other stuff done."

"Then ask another one of your love-sick losers to help, but not him."

Paul's left hand squeezed Sadie's chapstick, even while the pointed edge dug painfully into his skin.

"We have an exam next week, so I need to see him one more time before then," Sadie said, her voice hushed. "But after that, consider him gone. I promise it will be like I never knew him."

● ● ● ● ● ●

The window of Paul's dorm room glowed into the evening and past midnight. He sat in bed with several pillows behind him as he slipped into another hour of DNA research and hypothesis. The lamp on his desk cast heavy shadows around the small room where he lived alone and frequently dove into long hours of obsession with his scientific theories.

After Paul finished typing a paragraph of notes, he stared at the document, wondering how he could best manipulate the DNA of a living person without any negative side effects, or death.

If a surgeon can cut and reshape the skin to improve beauty, then why can't it be done on a molecular level? Radiation can easily alter DNA... no knives or scars involved. All radiation is fatal in large doses. but maybe, it still could be the answer...

Paul sighed and closed his eyes, tilting his head back against the pillows. His right hand slid from the keyboard on top of Sadie's chapstick, which rested on the blanket covering him from the waist down. He squeezed the tube tightly against his palm again, his anger blooming as he remembered how Jordan had interrupted their perfect evening together.

Were it not for him, Paul knew he finally could have had her all to himself...

If I could change my DNA, I could make myself an exact physical copy of him, and Sadie... she'd love me then... she would never know the difference.

Paul's grip on the chapstick loosened as he lifted his head and sat up straighter. His anger faded while another memory crossed his mind, recalling a class where a professor had discussed the different types of known radiation—particularly ionizing radiation.

Paul grinned and opened another browser tab on his laptop, eager to let another hour or two pass as he explored its possibilities further.

Ionizing radiation changes DNA and a single large dose could alter all DNA sequences at once, transforming the body almost instantly at the cellular level... but preventing organ or bone marrow damage... I need to fix that.

By the time Paul fell asleep in the early morning hours, his notes had several new paragraphs about ionizing radiation, as well as a tall, cylinder-shaped machine to control and generate it, complete with a hollow, human-sized core.

4 - LURE

Paul watched Sadie discretely around campus the next few days, his anger softening as she failed to study biology on her own in the library. Her labored efforts ended with a frown and frustrated sigh—justifying his belief that Sadie needed *him* as much as he *needed* her.

To Paul, it mattered little how different their reasons were, and while he waited for Sadie to call on him again for the exam, he busied himself with another obsession—countless sketches of the newly imagined black, cylinder-shaped machine. His notes of how to build and operate it surrounded each drawing, but without the right tools or laboratory space, Paul knew it would be years before he could make the machine a reality.

Two days before the biology exam, he sat alone inside a study room at the library, detailing a sketch while rain struck the tall window beside him. His textbooks laid open across the table after a few hours of studying, and Paul lost himself in the machine until the door to the study room slowly creaked open.

He looked up suddenly, his eyes widening once he saw Sadie standing in the doorway.

"Hi Paul," she said, her tone shy and apologetic. "Do you mind if I come in?"

He shook his head, and Sadie stepped inside, closing the door behind her. She smiled a little and walked to the table, setting her backpack on top of it.

"I've been trying to do our biology homework by myself," she confessed, her gaze downward. "I just thought it would be nice to put in more effort and not take up your time, but... the exam is in two days, and I'm freaking out."

Sadie bit her lip and finally met his gaze, the calmness of her features fading into anxiety. Though Paul greatly enjoyed her failed efforts, his face only showed the disappointment she caused.

"Do you really want my help, Sadie?" he asked.

"Of course," she replied eagerly. "I finished the study packet today, but if you could look over my answers, then I promise to leave you alone and not bother you any more. You've been so kind and helpful, Paul."

Despite the sincerity that filled her voice and lay plain upon her face, the corners of Paul's mouth turned downward as his anger returned.

This time, he minded her lie, and he wouldn't let her get away with it.

"I can help you… but Sadie, you owe me."

"Owe you? What do you want?"

Paul rose from his chair without a word, his long stride taking him quickly to her side. Sadie took a small step back, her fear growing as she looked him in the eye.

"We need each other," Paul said, his voice hushed. "I need your beauty and perfection, Sadie—it's so intoxicating and satisfying in every way. I've never seen a woman so perfectly made and appealing to every instinct I have. Maybe one day I can be like you, and I know you need me, too, Sadie. My intelligence and money can take care of you—I promise to give you whatever you want. But… you broke my heart last night."

Sadie's face contorted and she tried to move away, but Paul slipped a hand behind her head, his fingers lacing through her hair to grip it tightly.

"You can't throw me away—not after all I've done for you. We need each other to be complete, and you will be *mine*."

Sadie gasped, her struggle against his hold hindered by his other hand grabbing her arm, and his lips meeting hers. Paul pressed his mouth firmly into hers, but Sadie soon broke their kiss, her scream causing him to let go of her in a flicker of panic.

"You monster!"

Paul felt no regret as tears filled her eyes, noticing Sadie's distress slightly weakened her beauty. Sadie turned and sprinted for the door, leaving her backpack behind as she fled into the main library.

● ● ● ● ● ●

Although Paul's dinner plate was empty, Becky had abandoned half of her burger and several fries while she listened intently to his story. Paul's gaze fell to his empty coffee mug once he finished, his hand balling into a fist again.

"When Sadie told Jordan about the innocent kiss… he and his friends beat me for it after my night class the next day. They dragged me into the woods and left me there unconscious. I woke up a while later, hardly able to see or move."

"Are you serious?" Becky replied with a gasp. "But she kissed you!"

Paul shrugged, frowning.

"Correct. But Jordan was jealous of my knowledge and how it impressed her," he said, his lie effortless. "Sadie had merely thanked me, and he couldn't handle it. When I got checked out, I had two broken ribs, a sprained wrist, and a lot of bruises... plus a concussion."

Becky's eyes widened as she stared, her mouth slightly open and seemingly unable to speak.

"I can't believe this," she said at length. "Did you report them to the police, or school security?"

Paul shook his head slowly.

"No. Jordan never touched me again... and Sadie... I felt even worse when she transferred to another college."

"Why did she do that?"

"She became very unhappy, and left without saying goodbye."

Becky frowned, sighing.

"You still should have reported the assault, Paul. Jordan and his friends shouldn't get away with that."

His sudden grin surprised her and triggered an unexpected chill down her spine.

"Don't worry, Becky. I'm very happy with how it all turned out."

She looked away and smiled a little, uncertain why it seemed best to take him at his word.

"I'm sorry you lost your parents and had to deal with that in college," she replied gently. "But everything has gotten a lot better since, right?"

"Yes, life has gone well," he replied steadily. "But you're part of that now, Becky. I'm so glad we met."

Her pale cheeks flushed as she smiled, her adoring gaze locked with his. Although Paul did enjoy their time together, her affections and sympathies would also be useful for drawing her closer to the machine.

"Maybe you'll cure cancer one day," Becky said with a small laugh. "You're certainly smart enough, and when you're famous, you'll get the respect you deserve."

Paul smiled, revealing his straight, though yellowed teeth.

"So, will you come for dinner at my house Friday night?" he asked, repeating himself from earlier.

Becky nodded quickly, her eyes full of excitement.

"Excellent, Becky. I can hardly wait. It will be the perfect night."

* * * * * *

Paul ate his bowl of cereal quietly while his father read the morning newspaper at the head of the dining table. Paul Sr. was well into his fifties with graying hair and a wrinkled face that easily revealed his friendly, natural charm. He wore a green robe and plaid pajama pants, and Paul sat near him wearing dark blue pajamas with brightly-colored planets that he had received for his twelfth birthday last month.

Sunlight from the large dining room window bathed both of them while they listened to Paul's mother Teresa talk excitedly in the kitchen. Paul Sr. could see her standing next to the fridge a short distance away while she held the red wall phone to her ear, letting the long, twisted cord sway and dangle in the air.

Teresa kept her brown hair in tidy curls, and she covered her tall, thin frame in one of her many sundresses because of the sunny June weather. Heavy make-up covered her face each day, and though most people politely ignored how it startled them, Paul Sr. hardly seemed to notice.

When the call ended a short time later, Teresa entered the dining room and slid down into her husband's lap, her arm resting across his shoulders. In the bright sunlight, Paul saw faint impressions of the long scars she tried to hide along her cheeks and jaw, but whenever he asked questions, he was told not to be concerned.

"The Governor is coming to the play!" Teresa announced happily. "He's been a huge fan of *Prairie Dreams* since he saw it on Broadway a decade ago, and I can hardly imagine *him* as a guest for my debut leading role! Who would have thought such wonderful things could happen to me."

Paul watched his parents kiss and then his father laughed affectionately.

"I'm so proud of you, Teresa," Paul Sr. said, grasping her chin between his thumb and index finger. "You've taught me that a man can't be satisfied without a beautiful, successful woman."

5 - TRAP

Friday night, Becky climbed into her car that sat parked in front of her parent's house. Her head still spun from the story Paul told about his college days, and as she started the engine, she tried to ignore the eerie feeling that crept through her.

She had no reason to believe she wasn't safe alone with Paul in his house—yet the hair on the back of her neck seemed to stand on end at the thought of it.

I need to stop watching scary movies. There is nothing wrong with Paul or our date tonight. He just needs someone who truly cares about him...

Becky backed out of the driveway onto the dark, empty road, her headlights shining through the thin wall of fog in the air. While she accelerated slowly, she wondered if Paul might officially ask her to be his girlfriend that night, or sometime soon. Although they had only had two dates so far, her shameless infatuation fueled her impatience.

Has he had a girlfriend before? He said he's twenty-five... so I doubt I'm the first.

The inside of her car glowed from the lights of the dashboard, and Becky glanced at the tall, shadowed pines along the road, her anxiety starting to simmer again. Earlier, Paul had insisted on an eight o'clock dinner, and although Becky agreed, she knew it would have felt more comforting to visit during the daylight. Paul lived almost a half hour from her parent's house, and when she was less than ten minutes away, her phone vibrated in her pocket.

Becky pulled it out quickly, seeing a text.

PAUL: Are you coming?

She glanced at the road before quickly typing a response.

BECKY: Yes. Almost there.

She dropped her phone in a cup holder and sighed, her nerves slightly frazzled.

I'm not late, he's just excited...

Minutes later, Becky turned off the main paved road and onto a winding dirt road. The eeriness that settled upon her earlier returned, but there was little she could do about it now. When Paul's mailbox and address sign suddenly appeared from the dark, Becky hit the brakes and slowly turned into his driveway. Paul's house—which was a large, beautiful log cabin—sat in a dense patch of pine trees a short distance away, brightly lit by several exterior lights. A wide porch spanned the front of the house, and the windows pleasantly glowed with half-closed curtains.

Despite feeling unnerved, Becky started to relax as she stared at the house, which seemed to beckon her warmly. After parking beside Paul's truck in front of the detached garage, she stepped into the brisk evening air and glanced around, then made her way toward the front door. But as she came within inches of the porch, the door opened with a loud creak, and Paul appeared in the doorway.

"Welcome, Becky," he said, his tone lively. "Did you have any trouble getting here?"

She smiled and shook her head, wishing her heart would stop pounding so much.

"It was very easy to get here," she replied. "But it is a little spooky at night."

Paul's grin widened as he turned sideways, his hand motioning for her to step inside.

"No need to feel scared. Dinner is almost done."

Becky nodded once and walked forward, quickly climbing the porch steps and passing inside the house. Beyond the door, the dining room was visible directly ahead, as well as part of the kitchen halfway between it and her. But as the delicious aroma of Paul's cooking put her at ease, she noticed the heavy thud of the door closing behind her, followed by the dull click of the dead bolt.

Becky took a deep breath and unzipped her jacket, her gaze flashing to a portrait of an older couple smiling happily on the wall to her left.

"Are those people your parents?" she asked, removing her jacket.

"Yes," Paul replied close behind her. "Hand me your coat, then wait for me at the dining table."

Becky turned and obeyed, the adoring look in her eye meeting his confident gaze. To her surprise, Paul's hand cupped the side of her jaw, causing a jolt of satisfaction to pass through her while his thumb stroked her cheek.

After they parted, Becky floated inside a dreamy haze as she made her way to the left end of the dining table and sat down. There, a white plate, silverware, and green place mat sat in front of her, along with a wine glass and three tall, flickering candles in the middle of the table. Becky reached for the Riesling bottle near her wine glass and pulled the cork, finding it already loosened. After filling her glass halfway, she took a sip and watched Paul in the kitchen.

He opened the oven and pulled out a large ceramic dish, then carried it toward her. The red dish was rectangle-shaped with a solid lid, and he set it on a wooden cutting board beside the candles.

"I can't wait for you to see my rabbits, Becky," Paul said quietly, though excited. "It's been a few weeks now and they're still doing quite well."

Becky smiled and raised a brow.

"Where are they? The living room?"

"No—they're in the basement, near the machine."

Despite a few sips of wine, Becky suddenly felt her throat run dry.

"The basement?" she asked, trying to hide her alarm. "You can't bring the rabbits up here?"

"Perhaps I could have, but you still need to see the machine."

Becky swallowed hard as Paul briefly returned to the kitchen and walked back with a black spatula. After lifting the ceramic lid, he pushed the edge of the spatula into the cooked lasagna, eventually placing a chunk onto her plate. While Paul cut his own piece, Becky bit her lip and sat up straighter as her muscles tensed.

"Becky... are you okay?"

"Yeah, I just—I hate basements."

Paul laughed a little, his hand gripping the Riesling bottle after setting down the spatula.

"You don't need to worry. My basement is very clean and bright—I spend most of my time home down there."

Becky nodded politely, unable to hide her small frown. Paul walked to his end of the table and sat down, changing the subject to a popular hiking trail an hour away. Becky managed to relax again as they shared their experiences on the trail, and before she knew it, both their plates and glasses were empty.

As she helped Paul clear the table, butterflies began to flutter in her stomach.

He's going to take me to the basement now... and I can't refuse again. Why didn't I realize this sooner? He must think I'm an idiot...

Once the table was cleaned, Becky followed Paul a short distance from the kitchen to a pale green door with splintered wood at the bottom. Paul grasped its golden knob and pulled the door open, flipping a light switch to reveal a long flight of wooden stairs leading downward. Becky crossed her arms defensively as he started into the basement, her pulse quickening.

But then she took a step, then another.

Each one became slightly easier until she found herself at the bottom, staring into a long room with a gray concrete floor and cinder block walls.

In the center, two large stainless steel tables sat a short distance apart, and wooden shelves lined the bottom half of the walls, filled with books, specimens, beacons, and other science-related objects Paul collected. The fluorescent ceiling lights kept the area very bright, but in a rush of horror, Becky noticed there were no rabbits, or DNA-altering machine.

"P-paul, where—"

"The rabbits and machine are in my private workshop through that door."

Becky's eyes shifted from his grin to the only door in the basement, positioned in the middle of the wall to her left. With a sigh, she hugged herself tighter.

"We have to go in there now?"

"Of course, Becky. Relax."

Paul reached for her closest hand, gently holding it in his own as she unfolded her arms. Becky smiled and met his gaze, comforted by his warm touch.

"Okay. Let's go in."

Her final submission pleased him, and once Paul opened the brown door, Becky took a breath and stepped inside.

6 - ALTER

Paul's private workshop was a rectangular-shaped room almost half the size of the main basement. A wooden countertop and open shelving ran along most of the wall space, and the same scientific clutter of the main area filled his private room. But a red blanket that covered a large square object on the floor—like a box—captured Becky's attention, until her gaze eventually drifted to a far more fascinating sight.

In the corner near the red blanket, a tall, cylinder-shaped machine stood, its glossy black surface reflecting the ceiling lights. Becky could hardly see how it opened or operated, but the tall machine hummed quietly beside a table, chair and computer.

Becky flinched when Paul's arm suddenly bumped hers as he walked by quickly, stopping within inches of the machine, which stood a few feet taller than him. He stared at it for a few long seconds, as if he could see endless detail that was invisible to her eyes.

"This is it, Becky... the DNA-altering machine," he said, his tone affectionate. "It can give you an entirely new life through controlled DNA mutations that can change anything about how you look. There is nothing else like it in the world."

His fingertips fell gently upon the smooth surface as Becky approached him, her anxiety fading while curiosity and wonder filled her. After stopping beside Paul, she touched the machine herself, surprised to find it slightly warm instead of cool.

"I didn't think it would be so big," she said thoughtfully. "Seems like you could put two people inside."

"No, only one," Paul replied. "Are you ready to see my first creations?"

Becky blinked, nodding.

"Sure. Where are the rabbits?"

Paul turned from the machine and bent down, grasping the red blanket before he ripped it away to reveal a gray-wire cage. Inside, Becky saw a brown rabbit-like creature that wheezed and twitched while it sat alone on the left side of the cage.

She gasped as she studied it, seeing that it had tall, erect ears like a normal rabbit, but its eyes were milky-white and bloodshot. A few pointed teeth were exposed outside of its predator-like snout, and the creature's limbs were also elongated with crooked, yellowed claws jutting out from its paws. Becky noticed the fur around its mouth looked dark and wet, and in the middle of the cage, she saw two more grotesque rabbits lying dead, their bodies twisted and torn.

"Why did you kill them?" Paul suddenly barked, kicking the cage. "All of you were special to me!"

The demented creature leapt at the cage bars and hissed while Paul glared at it, and Becky shook her head, hardly to speak or think.

"I don't understand this, Paul. What have you done?"

His anger faded as he looked at her and a pleasant smile returned.

"Don't be upset, Becky—*please*. I know my rabbits aren't beautiful, but that's not what they need to be happy or survive. They need to be fierce like the predators that kill them."

Becky furrowed her eyebrows, unable to ignore the ugliness of his obsession which made her pulse race.

"You shouldn't do this, Paul," she said, her voice shaking. "You shouldn't care so much about physical appearance. You're ruining the balance of nature and not everything is meant to be the same. Beauty and strength is found in all different ways to people and in nature. Our lives are not limited because we weren't born to be on the cover of a magazine!"

Tears stung at Becky's eyes as she took a step back from Paul and the cage, but he strode to her and gripped the sides of her arms.

"There is never an advantage to imperfection," he replied coldly, his gaze piercing hers. "Didn't you hear me at the diner? I loved Sadie more than her boyfriend ever could—I adored her and would have given her anything she asked for—but my physical flaws repelled her. There *is* a standard of perfection and beauty that people like you and me are too far from... including my own mother. Don't you know she'd still be alive if she were beautiful?"

Becky blinked, her gaze held captive inside Paul's while a new horror filled her.

"Paul, what..."

"Don't you want to be perfect and beautiful?" Paul asked, the firmness of his voice and expression softening. "I can do that for you, Becky... I can make you so happy and change the rest of your life."

Becky stared at him in wonder, her thoughts entertaining the allure of such an offer. But she could still hear the hissing of the demented rabbit, and a heavy weight in her gut warned her against stepping inside the strange machine. She closed her eyes as the tears that threatened to spill out earlier fell onto her cheek.

"I'm sorry, Paul—I can't do it," she replied quietly. "Maybe I'll never be as beautiful as you desire, but I can accept my imperfections. I want to go home now."

Paul sighed and Becky felt soothed when his hand left her arm to rest gently upon her cheek, his thumb stroking her skin slowly.

"This is your home, Becky. And you will always be beautiful to me."

Before she knew what to do, Paul grabbed her shoulders and pulled her to the ground, immediately straddling her. Becky screamed until his hand covered her mouth, and he pinned one of her arms beneath his knee. Paul then pulled a capped syringe from his pocket and popped off the cap with his thumb.

"You will thank me, Becky, I promise," he insisted excitedly. "This will help you relax before our new life together begins."

Becky could hardly move as the sharp tip of the needle pierced the side of her neck, her mouth still covered. But not more than a minute passed before she began to feel dizzy and her vision darkened.

Why did I... she thought, her mind drifting from consciousness. *Why did I let this all go wrong?*

● ● ● ● ● ●

Paul waited until her eyes closed and all tension left her body before he finally stood up. He stared at Becky's limp form for a few long seconds—hardly able to believe that he finally had a human test subject. But her altering meant more to him than anyone else.

You don't know what's best for you, Becky...

Paul squatted and scooped her in his arms, then carried her toward the black machine. After pressing a flat button near the door, it popped open a few inches and Paul pulled the door back easily, revealing the white, hollow core. Fluorescent lights were spread out along the inner curved wall, and multiple cylindrical collimators were attached to it on rotating bases, all of which pointed at the thin metal slab in the center. The shiny slab stood upright with a backward tilt, and Paul carefully laid Becky on it, then secured her body with leather straps around her wrists, waist, and ankles.

When he finished, he stood back and grinned, thoroughly delighted.

After closing the machine door, Paul walked a few feet to a computer and sat down, opening a program from the desktop. The program interface showed a black, empty area on the left, and had multiple controls and gauges on the right. Paul clicked a button that read SCAN in red letters, and within minutes, a 3D-model of Becky's body filled the black area of the interface.

It was then Paul began to sculpt the model to his liking—adjusting the color, length, and size of several parts of Becky's body through clicks and manual commands. But once he had carefully recreated her from head to foot, he triggered the radiation accelerators to begin Becky's extraordinary transformation.

7 - PERFECT

The chill of cold metal bit at Becky's skin while she slowly woke to consciousness again.

She squinted at bright lights above her while trying to make sense of where she was or what had happened—but her mind felt clouded and blank. Becky's fingers twitched as her hands lay beside her hips, and through her mental fog, the eerie image of a syringe formed a few minutes later.

"Becky, my love... how do you feel?"

A black silhouette suddenly blocked the bright light above her, but within seconds, the details of Paul's face became clear. Becky sighed in relief and pressed one of her hands to her forehead.

"Paul... I feel fine, but what happened? Why am I—"

"You have nothing to worry about anymore. Come see how perfect you are."

Becky blinked, her eyebrows furrowing in confusion. Paul smiled and took her hand, helping her into a sitting position and eventually off the table. Becky frowned as the cold cement floor felt uncomfortable to her bare feet, but she said nothing as Paul guided her to another part of the basement with his arm around her waist. But as they walked, a sense of panic started to fill her as fractured memories returned—gruesome rabbits; the prick of a needle; her mind spinning before she slipped into darkness.

"What happened to me, Paul?"

Worry and desperation filled her voice, but Paul then halted, bringing them to an abrupt stop. Becky stared at him as her heart pounded, eagerly waiting for some kind of answer—but he seemed not to notice.

"Look at yourself."

Becky blinked and followed his line of sight, which peered into a full length mirror in a corner near the staircase. The glass rested in a black frame, but it reflected Paul and another woman she had never seen before—a woman with more beauty than she could imagine. The stranger had full lashes and striking blue eyes above plump lips and hollow cheeks, along with wavy black hair that fell to her waist. Her tall and slender body was clothed in a red dress that had thin shoulder straps and a gently pleated skirt which ended at her knees. The classy look contrasted sharply with the dingy basement, as well as Paul's green plaid shirt and brown pants.

Becky took a step forward while entranced with wonder—surprised to see the unknown woman mimic her move. But the moment she understood the truth, she gasped and stumbled back.

"How does it feel to be perfect?"

The pleasure in Paul's husky voice made the hair on her arms rise, and Becky turned to face him, tears brimming her eyes.

"How does it feel? I remember now... you convinced me to come down here even though I didn't want too, and then you—you *forced* me down and *drugged* me."

Paul's face filled with sympathy as he quickly closed the space between them, his hands holding each side of her face.

"You had to experience what the machine could do for you," he insisted. "I'm sorry I had to scare you, but your life is *perfect* now. Beauty is everything in this world."

Becky bit her lip as a few tears escaped, her hands gripping the front of Paul's shirt.

"Maybe it does mean a lot to some people... but I learned to love my body the way it was."

Paul's sympathy drained from his face as Becky waited for him to respond—perhaps apologize, though her gut told her otherwise.

"I'm certain you don't want it back, correct?"

Becky sighed heavily, her inner defeat clear by the look in her eye.

"No... I don't."

"Precisely. I made no mistake, Becky. You simply didn't understand."

"Is it permanent?"

"Yes."

Paul's hands slid from her face to her hips, and Becky leaned against him, resting the side of her face on his chest.

"How do I explain this new body to my parents, or friends?" she asked. "What if they don't believe anything I say? I don't want to give up my whole—"

"Stop, Becky—I told you not to worry. It's very late. We can talk about it tomorrow."

Her anxiety faded as she realized any concept of time had slipped her mind, but her attention returned to Paul as he took one of her hands and kissed it.

"You are a dream, a lovely dream... and I love you."

Becky smiled, her heart racing from three words she could hardly imagine had left his mouth.

"I love you, Paul. You're such a genius and performed a great miracle on me. But you said it's late, so... will you show me to bed?"

Paul grinned, his eyes lively as he nodded.

"Yes, of course."

• • • • • •

A bright ray of sunlight through the gap of dark curtains woke Becky the next morning. She groaned and shifted beneath the bed sheets with a small smile as memories of her exhilarating night with Paul began to fill her head. And when she rolled over to bring herself closer to him, his side of the bed was empty.

Becky sighed and slid her hand to where he had lain during the night, drumming her fingers lightly against the mattress. While other memories returned that were not as pleasant, she didn't consider her new life horrible now, or even bad—for as Paul had said, she simply didn't understand before what he was trying to do.

But now... the fantasy had come to full bloom.

Becky pushed aside the covers and climbed out of bed, walking past her dress on the floor toward a green robe that hung from the bathroom door. She swiftly covered her bare body with it and glanced around Paul's bedroom, which she had paid little attention to the prior night. The entire room had orange paneling from top to bottom, and a yellowed square-shaped light fixture in the middle of the ceiling. An old brown dresser with a large picture of pine trees and fog-covered mountains above it sat near Paul's side of the bed and bathroom, and on the other side of the room, there was a desk stacked with books and a window mostly covered by curtains.

Becky considered his room quite bare compared to the basement, though it was there he spent most of his time. She left the bedroom and entered a dark hallway that led her to the living room, where she found Paul sitting on the couch. Although the faded blue piece of furniture sat parallel to the hallway, Paul looked in the opposite direction of her at the box TV set. He wore a white tank top and blue boxers, and Becky raised a brow when she spotted his glasses on the coffee table in front of him.

"Good morning, Paul."

Briefly startled, he looked at her.

"Good morning, Becky," he replied. "How did you walk out here so quietly?"

"I'm not sure... I guess you made me extraordinarily graceful, too."

Becky grinned and made her way to him, sliding down onto an empty cushion. She bent one of her legs beneath her and hung the other over the side of the couch, exposing it from the robe. Paul's hand fell upon her knee, and he stroked her smooth skin with his thumb.

"It's a shame you're farsighted," Becky said quietly with a sly smile. "It would have been nice to have your glasses off most of the night."

"Yes... absolutely, Becky."

"Can't your machine fix that?"

Paul's gaze shifted to hers while Becky imagined what *he* might look like after transforming inside the DNA-altering machine.

"Of course," Paul replied quietly.

"When will you go inside it?"

"Inside it? I can't. It's complex to operate."

"You could teach me."

His eyes lingered on hers as Becky stared at him eagerly.

"You need breakfast."

Paul rose from the couch and walked a short way to the kitchen, though Becky soon followed behind him. At the breakfast bar, she sat on a stool and watched Paul while he took several items out of the fridge. Although he had failed to answer her question, she decided to let it go for the time being.

"What's for breakfast?" she asked.

"Corned beef hash and eggs."

"Oh—impressive. I hardly know how to cook. Do you do it a lot?"

"Yes."

Becky placed her elbow on the counter top and rested her chin on her palm. Except for the noises Paul made, she noticed the quietness of the house, and how almost everything seemed to exist within a dull, yellow haze. Eventually, her gaze settled on the portrait of Paul's parents near the front door, and the mystery of the subtle scars on his mother's face intrigued her again.

"Paul… there's something I've been wondering about your mother."

Becky's heart pounded as she hoped the subject wouldn't offend him, and her tension grew when he didn't immediately respond. Paul stirred thin slices of potato and onion with a spatula inside a black skillet, and when he slowly turned a few minutes later, his expression was noticeably grave.

"What is it?" he asked.

"Oh, well, um—what was her name?"

"Teresa."

"Okay, thanks."

Becky dropped her gaze to the counter top as she lost her nerve to ask about the marks, but Paul seemed to have read her mind.

"Did you see the scars on her face?"

"Yes, but…"

"I never knew what happened until I turned sixteen, and then my father told me."

Becky's eyes widened, her anxiety taking a new turn.

"My mother's first marriage was to a man that did terrible things to her for years. She did a lot to try to stop his abuse—including going to a plastic surgeon to make herself beautiful. But they didn't have much money, and the one she went too wasn't very good—in fact, he was a sham, and left those long, *ugly* scars on her face."

Becky's mouth slightly opened, though she hardly felt able to respond.

"But that's not all, Becky. You see, my mother dreamed of being a theater actress, and after she married my father, he convinced her to start auditioning despite the scars. Fortunately, it worked out well for her—she was cast in many shows from the time I was born until *Prairie Dreams* years later. And that's when everything changed."

Becky frowned while her blood raced, and a strange, lively energy came into Paul's eyes.

"*Prairie Dreams* was her favorite play since childhood and she finally had the chance to star in the lead role. My mother was certainly talented, but the theater director was sympathetic to her past and she had known him for years. Unfortunately, he was old, Becky, and had a heart attack three weeks before the show. The new director that came didn't know my mother or care about what the role meant to her. He dismissed her for not fitting *his* vision and her understudy starred in the show instead. Of course, my mother was devastated, and later learned that he didn't think she was beautiful enough for the role—with or without the scars."

Becky squeezed her eyes shut and placed a hand over her mouth as the cruel tragedy sunk in.

"I remember the morning she got the role," Paul continued. "I was eating breakfast with my father when she answered the call, and I remember how happy she was—how happy we *all* were. But she wasn't born beautiful, and in the end, it ruined her."

Becky opened her eyes and took in a deep breath before furrowing her eyebrows.

"It ruined her? What did you mean when you said your mother would still be alive if she was beautiful?"

Paul's lively energy faded as his expression returned to being grave and withdrawn.

"She died from an accidental overdose, Becky—at least, that's what the coroner's report said. She'd taken antidepressants for years... but a few months after she lost the role, she took too much."

Becky broke their shared gaze, casting hers down at the countertop. While the intentional suicide of his mother seemed quite possible to her, she could hardly accept the lack of beauty being the sole cause. But her thoughts were interrupted when Paul suddenly appeared beside her, his hand cupping her jaw as he lifted her face.

"Every advantage is yours now," he said quietly. "You will never suffer like that—ever."

Becky blinked as she tried to understand him, but despite the confidence in his eyes, his words only sounded like a delusion.

"You think your mother's life was tragic because of her looks? Cruel people hurt anyone, Paul—it doesn't matter what you look like. I think your mother needed a lot of help to cope with what she went through, but never got it."

Becky waited eagerly for a spark of revelation to pass through him, but Paul only stared at her, his gaze increasingly cold.

"I did you a favor," he said angrily. "And if my mother were here, I'd do it for her, too."

Becky made a skeptical noise in her throat and pulled away from him, sliding off the stool and taking a few steps backward.

"You did me a favor? You really did it for yourself! Every idea you have about beauty and its advantages are horribly warped."

Although her anger burned, Becky felt overcome by surprise when Paul lunged at her and gripped her throat, painfully restricting her breathing.

"Don't tell *me* I'm wrong—you're the one who can't see the truth clearly. My mother needed much more than sitting in a counseling office every week, and it's disappointing how stupid you really are, Becky. Can't you see how I've solved the fundamental problem for both sexes? All women want to be beautiful, and all men want to have a beautiful woman! You can't deny it and it tormented my mother. She was never good enough and neither were you before I put you inside the machine!"

Paul released Becky and shoved her to the ground, his fury keeping each muscle tense and his body rigid. He watched Becky cough and try to regain her breath as she sat up, though her hair shielded her face from view.

The impulse to comfort her then failed to dissolve his coldness, and he decided she deserved her punishment, even if his anger had temporarily broken his usual calm and calculated state. After a few seconds, he turned and took loud, heavy steps toward the basement, slamming the door behind him.

8 - ILL

Paul sat in front of his computer in the basement and tugged his hair while staring at the screen. His anxiety had been difficult to hide from Becky all week, and though she had mentioned his irritability a few times, he never admitted what bothered him.

Paul's gaze eventually drifted to the empty wire cage that used to contain his last genetically-altered rabbit. Although it had survived much longer than the others, a week had passed since he found it dead.

The radiation destroyed its bone marrow after all... but my tests showed nothing abnormal about it for weeks. Why did the poisoning take effect when everything looked healthy?

He sighed angrily at the computer, his eyes skimming paragraphs explaining clinical and natural methods of bone marrow restoration. The last rabbit had survived two months before its sudden death, and if Becky were to ultimately be affected the same way... he knew she only had about three weeks left.

She won't ever know about the poisoning—she doesn't have too. As long as she gets the right dose of proteins, vitamins, and other essentials... she'll live. I can make the medicine she needs.

Paul grabbed a pen next to the keyboard and scribbled a list of natural substances for bone marrow repair into his notebook. But his mind was hardly eased, for a lot of precious time to test a remedy had been lost while the rabbit appeared healthy, and many doses over a long period of time were likely required for successful treatment. But time was not what Becky had. And unlike the rabbit, she had already begun to show signs of illness.

A muscle in Paul's jaw tightened as he remembered the spontaneous bloody noses she had in the last few weeks, along with mild bouts of coughing and fatigue. Despite her suspicion that it was related to the transformation, Paul tried to tell her otherwise, however—she was never fully convinced.

When the door to his private workshop opened, Paul swiftly looked to his right, seeing Becky peek at him around the side of the door. After turning off the computer monitor, he looked back and saw her standing in the open doorway.

"It's boring upstairs—I can't watch any more television," Becky said. "When are you coming up? It's almost nine o'clock."

Paul closed his notebook and stood, shrugging casually despite his racing pulse.

"I'm done now, Becky. Let's go upstairs."

"What were you doing?"

"Researching my next project."

Becky nodded once, her gazing shifting suddenly from Paul to the wire cage, which sat fully covered by the red blanket and had been for some time.

"Your little pet is very quiet lately," she said curiously. "Is everything alright with it?"

"Of course. It's just sleeping."

"Okay. I want to see it."

Paul's nerves intensified as Becky took a step forward, but he cut her off while he walked toward her.

"I don't want it to wake up," he said firmly. "Let's go back upstairs."

"Come on, Paul—so what? It'll go back to sleep once we leave and shut off the—"

Becky gasped as a thin red line trickled down from her left nostril. She immediately pinched her nose with two fingers and Paul grasped her arms, his brow furrowing in concern.

"My third one today," Becky said, her tone shaken.

"Don't worry—it will all be okay," Paul said softly. "The air has been very dry for weeks, and your new body is sensitive to it. That's all."

"What about the coughing and exhaustion?" she asked. "It can't just be allergies, Paul—I think the machine did something bad to me, and that's the real reason why you won't go inside it. What did it do? What's wrong with me?"

Tears filled Becky's eyes and Paul sighed.

"Relax... take a deep breath," he said gently. "I have exciting plans for your birthday next week, and that's all I want you to think about."

Becky stopped pinching her nose and buried her face into Paul's chest, not caring that her blood stained his shirt while her arms laced around him.

"I can't wait," she replied quietly. "I'm sure I'll cherish this one the most."

Paul's face brightened as he smiled.

● ● ● ● ● ●

The morning of her birthday, Becky woke to a small velvet box on the nightstand beside her. Inside it, she found an oval sapphire sitting at the end of a delicate rose-gold chain. The depth of its dark reddish-pink color captivated her from the moment she saw it in a jewelry store a month ago, and she felt delighted that Paul had remembered her mentioning it.

After a shower and getting dressed, Becky wore the necklace to her all day spa retreat, which Paul had surprised her with after breakfast. When he picked her up at dusk, Becky expected to return home, but Paul took several unfamiliar turns until they drove down a dirt road that led into the thick darkness of the mountains.

"I promise nothing will be spoiled if you tell me where we're going," Becky said with a smile. "I've had plenty of wonderful surprises today."

Paul squeezed her hand as he held it on the empty seat between them, his gaze out the windshield.

"We're almost there," he said happily. "You can wait a little longer. I should have brought you your red dress. It would look stunning with the sapphire."

"I think my white dress makes it pop a bit more," Becky replied. "Will I get dirty where we're going?"

Paul smiled and shook his head.

"Not at all. Our destination is just around that turn ahead."

A minute later, Paul guided the truck around a gradual right turn in the road, but when they reached a dead end soon after, he pulled off into a grassy patch and parked. The dim headlights revealed a dark body of water close by, and Paul told Becky to wait while he climbed out of the truck. From the truck bed, he grabbed a folded blue blanket, a small cooler and a black bag that he carried to the area of grass between the truck and water.

Paul spread out the blanket and put the cooler and bag on top of it, then motioned for Becky to join him. She grinned and shut off the truck before she left and eagerly made her way to him. The silence of the dark mountain felt peaceful to her as she sat beside Paul on the blanket, and while he lit several small candles, Becky stared at the beautiful stars above them.

"Ready to dine, my love?"

"Dine?"

"Yes. I prepared several dishes while you were away."

Paul reached for the cooler and withdrew two chilled wine glasses, along with a clear wine bottle. After filling each glass halfway with apricot Riesling, he took out a large ceramic dish of baguette slices topped with cream cheese, a cucumber, and a fold of smoked salmon.

"Those look terrific," Becky said softly. "Should we toast before we begin?"

"Certainly," Paul replied, grinning as he lifted his wine glass in the air. "Becky, you are an absolute treasure. May you look and feel twenty-four forever."

She smiled and touched her wine glass to his, and together they took a long sip of Riesling.

"I think I might also add—"

A sudden cough wracked Becky's body and interrupted her, causing her to fight for air. Her wine glass fell to the blanket as she covered her mouth with her hands, her throat feeling noticeably warm and wet. Paul set her wine glass on the cooler and gripped her shoulder, his heart pounding in surprise.

"Just relax, Becky—slow, even breaths."

Becky stopped coughing a minute later and dropped her hands to her lap, though Paul noticed a shiny fluid across her palms. Her ragged breathing frightened him as she sat with her eyes closed, focusing her energy on each controlled inhale.

"Why blood?" Becky asked, rasping. "Why am I coughing up—"

She took a sharp breath before lurching forward, vomiting a small pool of blood on her lap that stained her white dress. Without another thought, Paul pulled Becky to her feet and scooped her in his arms.

"We're going to the hospital now!"

Becky continued to cough with her face against his chest, blood spattering across the front of his gray dress shirt. But before Paul could make it to the truck, her head suddenly fell back, and her hoarse breathing stopped.

"Becky? Say something!"

Paul dropped to his knees and cradled her while he tilted her head back up. Becky's eyelids fluttered as she tried to look at him, but her chest was barely rising.

"Paul..." she muttered. "Tonight... it was so wonderful."

Despite his urge to get her to the hospital, he knew her inevitable death had come, and it cruelly left him without any way of stopping it. Tears slid down his cheeks as Paul tore off his glasses, then held her tightly with his face buried in her neck.

"I hope..." Becky whispered. "I'm still... beautiful."

Her body jerked a few times as a gagging sound escaped her throat, but after that, she lay limp in his arms. Paul wept loudly in the dark for a while as he refused to let her go, his face smeared with tears and blood.

DARK BEAUTY

DANA

1 - CRASH

The pale blue evening sky eventually faded into thick darkness as I drove alone on a paved road that weaved through the mountains. Ordinarily, I might have worried about something bad and unpredictable happening, but instead, my thoughts obsessed over the honors club retreat I'd been on that weekend.

The majority vote chose Lake Tahoe as our fun get-a-way trip to celebrate the end of our spring semester, and although camping was fun and the lake was beautiful, I felt nothing but sour and disappointed most of the time. While everyone in my honors club swam in the water and played games, I sat alone on the beach in a one piece and wrapped in a towel, pretending to read a book I had brought.

The nine other people in my club had perfect bodies I wouldn't dare compete with—or at least, their bodies were a lot more perfect and attractive than mine. But the worst offenders to my insecurities were Ashley and Brynn, two of the three most perfected bodies of the group. The other belonged to Ethan—the crush of almost every girl it seemed, including myself.

For several days I sat on the beach watching as the three of them laughed, talked, swam and developed beautiful tans under the sun. I wished I could be so flawless and carefree, but unlike them or anyone else in honors club, I was sixty pounds overweight, though it looked like an extra one hundred and fifty pounds.

I sighed heavily as my gaze left the visible road in my headlights and fell on a half-eaten candy bar in the cup holder beside me. It felt like a sign of how hopeless I was, for not only did candy add the extra fat to my body that I loathed, but excessive sugar also functioned as one of my few sources of emotional relief.

I sighed heavily—again.

Weight wasn't even close to my only imperfection, though.

Crooked, yellowed teeth...

Thin, dull hair...

Blotchy, pimpled skin...

Sparse lashes and shapeless lips...

Should I ever show my face in society again? Who wants to look at me if I'm so ugly?

I felt a destructive urge to glance at my face in the rear-view mirror, but avoided it.

Straight, white teeth...

Full, shiny locks...

Clear, glowing skin...

Thick lashes and full lips...

None of these I had. But Ethan, Ashley, and Brynn did. And I knew Ethan would never hang out with me or gaze in the same adoring way that he did toward Ashley and Brynn without them. Or I guess, as he might with any other girl in existence, but not me.

Not ever.

I just want to be beautiful and never wake up hating myself again...

I stared at the empty road while it slipped away beneath me, wishing personality alone would be enough to convince Ethan to ask me out. But the painful, obvious truth was that it was rarely enough for anyone.

I grabbed the candy bar in my cup holder and finished it, deciding I might as well get whatever happiness I could in that moment.

I've never had a single date and I'm twenty-two now. How pathetic am I? Life just isn't fair unless you're pretty...

Even if I had to be ugly and never go on a date with Ethan, writing in my diary was another source of relief from any of my harsh realities. The top corner of it poked out of my large beach bag in the passenger seat, but like sugar... even journaling had negatives to its benefits.

I was honest about what I wrote—far too honest, maybe. If someone ever read it, they'd know all my loathing and *possibly* ridiculous but undeniable feelings I had toward myself. They'd know how much I ached to be beautiful, but could never be in the way I truly wanted. Although I could lose weight and get a makeover, I was never going to be as attractive as Ashley or Brynn.

Ultimately, I was trapped in a horrible body.

Nothing would ever change that.

I turned up the quiet radio in an effort to escape my dark mental spiral, but soon, two bright headlights distracted me as light flooded every inch of my car. My heart pounded as I realized a large truck had suddenly appeared at my bumper, causing me to wonder why the driver chose to tailgate me on an empty road.

Is it a serial killer? There's nothing I can do, except pretend like I don't notice and keep driving...

The daunting headlights filled my car until the unknown driver roared the engine and passed me a few minutes later. I sat like a statue and stared ahead stiffly as the truck drove alongside my car and eventually cut in front of me. When my headlights illuminated the back of the vehicle, I saw it was red and white, but also decades-old and rusted. The driver quickly got ahead of me and vanished after a few bends in the road, much to my relief.

I sighed and felt thankful just to breathe again.

What a jerk! Who drives like that at night?

My hands gripped the steering wheel hard while I worked to calm myself. My college dorm was less than thirty minutes away, and I planned to curl up like a frightened child beneath my blankets once I got there. But as I continued to follow the curves of the road, my calming efforts were hindered by sudden rain striking the windshield.

Why now?

I squinted as I tried even harder to see the dark landscape around me, and before I had much time to react, I saw a buck standing only yards in front of me in the middle of the road.

I screamed and instinctively swerved.

My car fell off the left side of the road within seconds, my brakes useless while I plummeted into countless plants and brush. Another scream left my throat as I had no idea how far I would fall, but my seat belt stopped my head from hitting the windshield while my body was thrown around. After a minute, a large enough bump threw me against the side of car, where my head collided with something very hard and precise.

I wasn't aware of anything after that.

Not even the consuming darkness of my own subconscious.

2 - BEAUTY

I drew in a deep breath as I squinted, blinded by another bright light in front of me, or even somewhere above. As far as I could tell, I wasn't dead, nor did I feel injured in any way. But fragments of driving and rain and falling circled my mind without clarity.

I closed my eyes again, taking a few minutes to clear my head before I noticed the soft blanket beneath me. Eventually, I turned my head slowly to the right, squinting again as I observed a variety of objects—notebooks, beacons, green bottles, small tools—on a long, steel table a few feet away.

What is this place? Why can't I remember anything?

I sighed and opened my eyes fully, which were now adjusted to the bright fluorescent ceiling lights above me.

Beyond the steel table, the rectangular cinder block room had open shelves that held books, jars, specimen samples, plants, and other items of a science-like nature.

I took a deep breath and pulled myself upward into a sitting position, realizing I was also on a long, steel table. My gaze flashed around the strange, basement-like room again, which I noticed had no windows and a staircase on the far right side.

Where am I? And... who brought me here?

Fear started to overwhelm me as I began to remember my life, family, and friends—all of which had no connection to this bizarre, unknown place. And I realized I had no memories of what happened after my accident, when my car fell into what seemed like a ravine before I lost consciousness.

While I resisted the urge to scream, I hugged my waist tightly—an innocent action that suddenly caused all emotion but surprise to drain from me. My eyes widened as I looked down at my waist, which was incredibly small and firm inside a simple, though elegant red dress.

I blinked in shock and quickly studied my arms and legs, which were long and also slender, but certainly *not* part of the body I remembered.

Did I go insane or am I dreaming? Is that why nothing makes sense?

I swung my legs over the side of the table, shivering when my bare feet touched the cold, cement floor. No matter what kind of reality I had slipped into, a desperation to escape it filled me, and the staircase on the right side of the room seemed to be the only way. But I hardly made it a few feet before a portrait on the wall at the end of the table stopped me.

I stared in awe at a beautiful young woman with long black hair who sat in an old leather chair in front of a white wall. Her hands were folded neatly in her lap while her legs were crossed, and I thought the look in her eye was slightly devious. Although I felt captivated by her beauty, my trance broke when I focused on her dress. It was red with thin straps and ended just at her knee—or in other words, the dress was identical to mine.

What the hell is going on?

A shiver ran down my spine while I stared at the large portrait, which stood out colorfully from the shelves and dull clutter around it. I inched closer as I grew curious about a much smaller picture frame beside it that held a newspaper clipping behind the glass.

The black-and-white image of a wrecked car was next to several paragraphs of small text, and after skimming, I realized the article reported the accidental death of a young man named Jordan Stoll.

I furrowed my eyebrows and looked away from it, unable to make sense of the portrait or article.

Everything keeps getting stranger...

My gaze shifted desperately to the staircase again.

I walked as fast as I could across the room toward it, but just as I reached the first step, I thought I caught a glimpse of someone else. My blood raced as I carefully looked to my left, where I felt sure I had seen something move. But there was nothing in that corner of the basement—just a full length mirror propped against the wall several feet away.

I blinked, realizing I must have seen my reflection as I quickly passed it.

Although I wanted to climb the stairs, the chance to see what my face looked like became too tantalizing to ignore. I took a few steps back and turned to the mirror, walking slowly toward the glass.

I noticed my thin, dull hair had been replaced by long, glossy locks while I approached, and soon, I stood close enough to stare into my alluring brown irises that rested beneath thick eyebrows and lashes. The shape of my eyes, nose, lips and jawline were perfectly delicate, and the faint red tinge in my cheeks completed the impossible beauty of my flawless complexion. The rest of my body—as I had already discovered—looked just as sculpted and enviable.

If I am crazy, I don't care anymore. I am so beautiful now—more beautiful than anyone I've ever seen, and not even Ethan could get a date with me now...

The basement seemed to disappear as I twirled and posed in front of the mirror, filled with a kind of happiness I had never known before. Everything about my new body was so perfect, thin, and soft that I no longer wanted to leave whatever unexplainable reality I had slipped into.

"You're so beautiful."

The calm, husky voice that filled the air made me stop modeling instantly.

On the left side of the mirror, I saw a man standing a short distance behind me in a newly opened doorway. His dirty blond hair fell into his eyes, which peered at me through wide-framed glasses. A patchy scuff covered his chin and jaw, and I noticed several red blemishes that stood out against his pale complexion. The strange man stood taller than me despite a slight hunch, and he wore a faded green t-shirt and blue jeans.

For a few long seconds, we stood in silence, though I wondered what to say or ask first.

"I'm Dana," I finally said, awkwardly. "And I just woke up a little bit ago, but... I have no idea where I am, or who you are."

The man nodded, his cryptic expression without surprise or concern.

"Are you hungry?" he asked.

I blinked, furrowing my eyebrows.

"What?"

"I'm sure you are."

"Well... a little, yes."

Without quite knowing why, I felt a sense of dread when I saw the corner of his mouth turn upward.

"Good—I was about to check on our dinner. You won't be confused for long. I will answer your questions."

● ● ● ● ● ●

The pleasant aroma of meat and herbs greeted me at the top of the staircase. The strange man had passed through the door first, but I lingered there, studying every part of his house I could see.

The unruly man busied himself not far away in the kitchen while I walked toward a dining table nearby. It had already been set for dinner, and I touched my grumbling stomach after I sat down.

How did he know I was hungry? And wait—did he dress me?

I didn't think about it for too long before the man emerged from the kitchen carrying a large, red ceramic dish. He set it in the middle of the table, and afterward, opened a wine bottle and filled my glass halfway.

"My name is Paul," he said gently. "This is my house, but you are welcome to anything you like here."

I smiled politely while he filled his own glass and sat down at the opposite end of the table. Although many questions burned inside me, I waited quietly as he served himself a chunk of lasagna, and then I did the same.

"I saved you from a terrible accident," he began, surprising me. "I saw your headlights in a deep ditch off the side of the road, and so I rescued you and brought you here."

"Oh—thank you," I replied. "I do remember that—falling into the ditch or ravine, I mean. But I can't explain anything else... like... how I look."

My gaze lingered on my slice of lasagna before I could bring myself to look at Paul. For some reason, I expected him to be confused and tell me I had always looked this way—but he ate quietly, as though I had said nothing at all.

"Yes... you are very different now," he finally replied at length. "I put you inside my DNA-altering machine, which made you perfectly beautiful and unharmed."

My eyes widened as I gasped, though my mouth remained open in shock.

"A *what* altering machine? How is that possible?"

"Anything is possible if you find the right method. I developed it at the research laboratory I used to work at before it was shut down."

"Shut down? Why?"

"Please, start eating. You need to."

I looked at my plate and robotically cut a small piece of lasagna, eating it while I nervously obsessed about the information he had shared with me. Despite how impossible a DNA-altering machine seemed for my transformation, it was the only explanation I had for any part of the bizarre reality I existed in since the accident. And as much as Paul put me on edge, he provided the only source of answers I could readily have.

"Don't you love how you look?"

His tone sounded curious and sincere.

"Yes—I'm very much in love with my new body," I said with a grin. "Even if I wake up in a padded white room tomorrow, at least I had one perfect moment in my life."

"I promise you're not crazy, but I agree... beauty is everything in this world."

Paul's satisfied smile unnerved me, and I took a long drink from my wine glass.

"Speaking of perfect beauty... who is the woman in the portrait?"

His expression darkened a little.

"Her name is Becky," Paul replied slowly. "But she died a year ago."

"Oh... I'm so sorry."

Was she also put inside the machine?

I bit my lip and chewed another piece of lasagna, uncertain if I should speak my thought out loud.

"I'll show you to your room when you're finished," Paul said, switching the subject. "I put all your things from your car in there."

"Thank you. Is it still in the ravine?"

"Don't worry. I took care of it."

I sensed I shouldn't press for more information, and I didn't feel comfortable with the idea of *my room*—especially for more than one night.

When we finished eating a short while later, I rose full and tired from my chair.

"I'm ready to go to bed now."

"Alright... this way."

Paul led me into the living room next to the dining area, and I followed him down a hallway to the first door on the left. When he opened it, I saw a bed in one corner beside a large window, and my suitcase and beach bag were sitting on top of the bed.

"There's a bathroom across the hall," Paul said softly. "Let me know if you need anything. You're in the safest place for miles."

"Good. Where's your room?"

"At the end of the hall, but I'm not going to bed yet."

He turned away and left me beside the open door, which I promptly entered and closed. I went to the bed and searched my things, finding my purse tucked inside the suitcase. I dug to the bottom of it for my cell phone, but when I pressed the power button, a dead battery icon flashed before the screen went black again.

I sighed and set it on the nightstand before I changed into my baggy pajamas, moving my suitcase and beach bag to the floor. After turning out the light, I unlocked the window and opened it a crack, then slipped beneath the bed sheets. For a while, I listened for any strange noises or Paul's footsteps, but soon, I fell asleep.

3 - TRUTH

I woke up to sunlight and a gentle breeze the next morning. All memories from the night before returned in a flurry, and I looked under the bed sheets, thrilled to see my body hadn't lost a touch of perfection. But a particular thought caused the smile on my lips to grow:

I'm going home today!

After pushing aside the covers, I sat on the edge of the bed, suddenly wondering how I would ever explain my transformation to my family—or anyone else, for that matter. The truth still seemed as impossible as when Paul had told me during our dinner, but all possible effects my new body might have on my life became far too much to consider right then.

I took a deep breath and knelt beside my suitcase on the floor, eagerly rummaging for some personal items I packed for the honors retreat.

Deodorant? *Check.*

Makeup bag? *Check.*

Straightener and blow dryer? *Check, check.*

Wait... where's my diary?

I furrowed my eyebrows and grabbed my beach bag, remembering I had tucked it between two towels. But after pulling the towels out, I found nothing but sunglasses and sunblock. I started emptying my suitcase then, but even after all my clothes and other items were removed, my pink leather diary remained missing.

I brought it to Lake Tahoe, right? I mean, I remember writing in it inside my tent, and I think I saw it before the accident...

I sighed and stood, frustrated more than I imagined. Because all my old clothes would no longer fit right, I changed back into the red dress and left the bedroom. I heard sounds in the kitchen as I walked through the hall and living room, and the smell of eggs and sausage filled the air. My stomach grumbled again when I reached the long counter top between the kitchen and dining room, and I sat down on the middle stool.

Paul's back faced me while he cooked at the stove, and I wondered if he was aware of my arrival or not. Like the night before, he wore a plain t-shirt and jeans.

"How did you sleep?" he asked, just as I opened my mouth.

"Um—just fine," I replied, slightly startled. "The bed was comfortable."

"Breakfast will be done soon."

I nodded and tried to wait for him to finish cooking, but the silence quickly felt awkward.

"Did you just flip an omelet?"

"Yes. I hope you like ham and green pepper. This one is made special for you."

"Oh... thanks."

I frowned slightly as the fine hair along my arms stood on end. Despite my gratitude for his rescue and my physical perfection, Paul's kindness created a slight sense of unease within me. I didn't mind the silence this time while I waited for him to serve the omelet and sausage, which he did only a few minutes later.

Paul leaned against the counter beside the stove as I ate and decided which questions to ask first.

"What is your last name?" I asked innocently. "I don't think I caught it last night."

"Henderson."

"Okay. I've also been wondering how I'm going to explain my new body to anyone?"

Paul crossed his arms and stared at me sternly through his glasses, which soon made my gaze drop to my plate.

"You won't need to explain anything to anyone, Dana. Everything you need is here."

I looked back at him and blinked, confused as to whether I had actually heard him correctly.

"What? Of course I have to explain this to my family and friends."

"No. You can't see anyone you used to know again. Like I said, everything you need is here."

My eyes widened while his words and their intent struck me fully that time. I stopped eating and slid off the stool, my heart thudding in my ears as I tried to understand the sharp twist of events.

"I have to see my family—I can't stay here. You can't *keep* me."

"I can, actually. Your life now depends on it."

I hardly knew what to say while I considered what that meant and my body shook. All at once I realized I had always been in some kind of trap—but it wasn't like anything I could imagine or predict.

"My life? Why..."

My voice sounded breathy and stressed, but there was nothing I could do to match his cold, unflinching facade.

"Remember the altering machine?" he said with a hint of excitement. "It changed your DNA through radiation, but I haven't completely figured out how to get around the fatality aspect, yet."

"You're lying! You can't be serious..."

"Quite serious. You'll live happily with me as long as you ingest Bioim powder to keep your bone marrow from dying quickly. You need healthy stem cells to stay alive, Dana."

My body felt paralyzed from the amount of shock and disbelief that coursed through me. As much as I wanted to believe he had told an insane, though clever lie, I couldn't dismiss it with the obvious proof of my own transformation.

"You can't keep me here no matter what you say. It's wrong—*cruel*—"

Paul's sudden move from the counter caused me to flinch and break my paralysis. I stared with dread as he approached, and much to my horror, he wrapped his arms around me, pulling my body against his.

"You wrote that you wanted to be beautiful more than anything else in your life, Dana," he said with a lively tone. "It's fate that brought us together, because now you can be beautiful *forever*... and I get to have a beautiful girl."

A depth of terror I had never known overwhelmed me as I realized *he* was the reason I couldn't find my diary earlier. But Paul had also invaded my thoughts and insecurities by reading it, and the words I so foolishly wrote across every page suddenly felt tragically empty.

"Did you do this to her?" I blurted, struggling uncomfortably in his hold. "Did you kill Becky with the machine?"

Paul's lively energy drained into gloom on his face.

"I loved her no less than I love you," he said. "But yes... I failed to save her. You don't need to worry, though. I wouldn't have damaged you if I wasn't certain the powder could keep you alive."

He raised his hand then, stroking my cheek with the back of his fingers. Mortified, I jerked my skin from his touch. Paul's gaze felt like ice slicing through me, and I doubted whether he had truly ever loved.

"Finish your omelet. It has all the powder you need for today."

• • • • • •

Despite my urge to escape, I decided to stay and fake submission to Paul in an effort to learn more about the Bioim powder.

Thankfully, he spent the majority of my first and second day in the basement working on an *exciting* project he wouldn't share the details of. And while he was busy, I mostly hid in my room, depressed and trying to think of a plan for my eventual escape *and* survival. Part of me also felt surprised by how little physical contact Paul seemed interested in having with me—though I hardly felt relief, for I wondered if his new project had anything to do with that.

He doesn't want a beautiful woman just to look at...

My blood raced at the implication of that haunting thought, but I finally had a boost of legitimate hope during our dinner my second night. While Paul cooked in the kitchen and I sat at the dining table flipping lazily through a magazine, I noticed a mason jar of pale green powder on the counter next to him. The sight of it almost made me jump from my chair as I wondered if that was the Bioim powder—and in such a large quantity—that I needed to live a life separate from him. But as difficult as it was not to ask, I didn't want him to think for a second that I might steal it and run.

Instead, I wanted him to believe I forever considered myself hopelessly dependent.

After breakfast my third morning, I hardly knew what to think when Paul lifted my hand and placed a dirty key and wad of cash on my palm.

"Take my truck and go into town," he said gently. "I can tell you've been unhappy, but it won't last for much longer. Let people stare at your perfection as you walk the street, and buy all the new clothes you like. My favorite will always be this red dress."

He pinched the red fabric of the skirt between his fingers while I tried to hide my repulsion.

"What if I don't come back?"

The question slipped out in the middle of my shock and confusion overwhelm.

Is this a trick?

"Think about it, Dana. You have no identity anymore, and there are many other reasons you will return to me."

Paul's icy stare and his cold smile appeared on his face before he turned from me and entered the basement. I stood between the kitchen counter and dining table while I wondered exactly what had or would happen. But eventually, I came to the sickening realization that there was no trick, because he was right.

The new body had erased any provable evidence of my life as Dana Carter.

4 - ESCAPE

Despite how difficult I found the drive from town back to Paul's house, the plan I had formed during my taste of freedom provided enough comfort.

And it wasn't that tricky, really.

I just had to be quiet—and somehow, fearless.

The metal door of his detached garage was still open as I pulled into the driveway and slowly steered his decades-old, rusted truck back into its spot. The garage had a dirty cement floor and walls covered by dark brown wood panels, as well as having dim light and a musty smell.

I climbed out of the truck and walked to the passenger side, grabbing a few clothes bags that slid from the seat onto the floor during the drive. When I had all of them looped around my arm, I shut the door and turned around.

My gaze immediately fell upon a green tarp that covered a large object in front of a yellowed, dusty window. The object seemed to have no particular shape I could make out, and it caused my curiosity to rapidly grow.

What would Paul hide under there?

I glanced around before I stepped toward the covered object, preparing myself for a possibly underwhelming discovery. But whatever it was stood a foot or so higher than me on one end, and the width of it looked as long as my body from head to toe. When I stood directly in front of it, I pinched a piece of the tarp and yanked downward, causing it to fall easier than expected.

The black, lifeless eyes of a buck stared back at me and sent a chill down my spine as I gasped and stumbled backward. Its stiff body looked incredibly lifelike, but its raised left foreleg began to disturb me.

The deer I almost hit... it stood perfectly still in the headlights, and it's leg—I swear it was raised—but this can't be the same one, because that would mean...

I shook my head and looked away from the deer. My sanity felt fragile again like when I woke in the basement, and I tried to imagine Paul somehow *staging* the taxidermy animal to cause my accident.

No, there's no way... this isn't the deer...

I looked back at the truck, though it did little to jog my vague memory of the other vehicle I knew had been on the road with me that night.

I left the tarp on the ground as I quickly left the garage and made my way back toward the house. The unsettled feeling in my gut subsided slightly when I walked through the front door, inhaling the delicious aroma of whatever Paul had made for dinner.

As I started walking to my room, I stopped when I saw him in the living room, his hand outstretched toward the large stereo next to the TV. Paul immediately looked at me, smiling while the lenses of his glasses gleamed.

"Come, Dana. I have a surprise for you."

Every muscle in my body tensed while I slowly set the clothes bags on the floor and approached him. My heart pounded when I glanced at his smile, wondering what horrible thing had excited him.

Paul pressed a button on the stereo just before I stopped a few inches away from him, and without a word, his hands grasped my waist and pulled me against him. I flinched as the front of our bodies met, hardly resisting the urge to push myself free of him. After lacing his fingers through one of my hands, he led me in a steady, rhythmic dance while classic music filled the room. But it wasn't just any composition—it was a piece I had listened to for a few years, and a particular fantasy of mine went along with it.

"Ethan never deserved you," Paul said, his mouth moving close to my ear. "I enjoy Nocturne as well, so it appears fate brought us together again, Dana. I will dance with you, and *we* will satisfy each other's longings."

I squeezed my eyes shut and hardly breathed.

Nothing could be worse than living life as Paul's prisoner... except for him to have direct access to my heart and mind, which he easily invaded through my much regretted diary.

"Did you have anything to do with my accident?" I blurted, though hardly above a whisper.

He didn't respond while we turned in a small circle, but his silence felt convincing of guilt.

"I rescued you and made you perfectly beautiful, Dana," he finally replied. "You should be very grateful."

"What about Jordan?" I asked, my voice starting to shake. "Did you have any part of *that* accident? Is that why you kept the article?"

Paul suddenly shoved me away, making a gasp escape my throat as I lost balance and nearly fell. But his painful grip on my wrist managed to keep me on my own two feet.

"Yes, I killed him," he said, his tone deep and heated. "He beat me up in college with his friends, and told Sadie to get away from me by transferring to another school. He thought I was pathetic, but he was extremely foolish, and that's why his brakes failed."

I felt unable to speak or think as I stared at him in greater horror than I ever had. I didn't know who Sadie was or how he had tampered with Jordan's brakes—but I also didn't want to. Paul struck the stereo behind him, stopping the music. I stood stiffly and said nothing while I watched his dark, upset expression fade back into its normally calm state.

"Think of me as a monster, but few people have the intelligence or ability to right the wrongs against them," he stated. "I will always find a way to solve my problems, even if the answer creates an ugly situation. But can you guess, Dana, the one problem I still have with *you*?"

My heart almost stopped when he finished speaking.

I dropped my gaze and shook my head, his grip on my wrist not loosening.

"I need your love and obedience, like I had with Becky. Fortunately, she offered both freely, but since her death, I've been experimenting with how I can get it automatically from any woman."

My eyes flashed back to his, knowing better than to believe it wouldn't be possible.

"Experimenting with what... an aphrodisiac?"

"No, a steroid. Androstadienone, specifically. It's already sold in colognes and fragrances for men because of its pheromone-like effects. For a year I've been trying to figure out the right dosage and form of application to alter a woman's brain chemistry and sexual desire to my advantage—far beyond some ridiculous *cologne*—and I think I finally have it. Your lovely assistance will be very helpful to me tomorrow."

"Is that why you haven't come after me yet? A good brainwashing stops any kind of fight."

"Precisely."

I frowned and tried to yank my wrist free, but Paul jerked me toward him, his free hand falling gently on my cheek. Despite my dark glare, his eyes studied my face without concern, and before I knew it, his cracked, rough lips pressed into mine. The few seconds our mouths met felt like an eternity in my shocked state, but it ended when Paul pushed me back again.

"Put your clothes away and get ready for dinner," he said with soft instruction. "I love you, Dana."

• • • • • •

Several hours after dinner, I stared at slivers of moonlight across the wooden floor while sitting on the edge of my bed. The courage I needed to explore Paul's house that night for the Bioim powder jar took longer than expected to muster up—but I'd seen the jar again on the counter earlier, and through conversation, Paul confirmed it to be what I suspected.

Although I wasn't exactly sure what he did with it once dinner ended, I assumed he had likely tucked it away in one of the cupboards.

I sighed heavily—still somewhat afraid to sneak around the quiet, dark house.

The purple t-shirt and jeans I wore were bought in town specifically for an escape attempt, which—because of the brainwashing pheromone—I knew *had* to be tonight.

No matter what.

I would rather die free than live as his mind-altered slave... that would be death, too, except in hell.

A chill ran down my spine as I imagined myself endlessly drugged by him, obeying without thought or concern whatever impulse satisfied him...

I practically jumped from the bed as the courage I needed surged through me. A while had passed since I heard Paul's footsteps move past my door and into his own bedroom. But he hadn't come out, and I hadn't heard any other sound.

Did he go to bed and fall asleep fast? I guess there's no way to know...

I slowly approached my door and opened it silently, peeking down the dark hall toward Paul's door. It stood closed with no light shining through the bottom gap, which assured me that he must be sleeping. After a minute, I finally slipped out into the hallway, sliding easily along the hardwood floor in my socks.

When I made it to the kitchen, I counted each cabinet with a glance—twelve total that I needed to search. I took a deep, silent breath and moved toward the first cupboard, gently opening it to look inside.

But, no jar of Bioim powder.

For almost ten minutes, I repeated this process until I opened the last one, feeling all hope drain from me as I was met with only cans and food boxes. Though it seemed convenient for Paul to leave the jar in the kitchen, I wondered if he had purposely hidden it now that I knew what lay inside.

I lingered in the kitchen while curiously glancing at the basement door a few times. If the jar wasn't in the kitchen, the next best place would be in Paul's private space below ground—but searching it would take a lot more time, and effort.

I sighed, torn.

I need to get out of here, but my life literally depends on that powder...

After another minute of debate, I finally moved toward the green door. The silence in the house continued as I wrapped my hand around the silver knob, twisting it. But a loud, short *creak* filled the air when I opened the door a few inches, causing me to stand rigidly while I listened.

Another door opening swiftly...

Footsteps running toward me...

Paul angrily shouting threats...

All of these I expected within seconds, but after the dreadful *creak*, there wasn't another sound in the house. I finally relaxed a little and pulled the door open fully with no more noise, then flipped the light switch above the stairs before I made my way down. At the bottom step, I turned right into the main room of the basement, my gaze fixed on the door that led into Paul's private workshop. Part of me felt stupid as I half-expected it to be locked in some way, but the door glided back easily once I turned the knob and gave it a small push.

While my gaze drifted across the room, I wasn't surprised to find it cluttered with books and other objects like the main area—even an odd and empty wire cage. But the hair on the back of my neck stood up when I focused on a tall, black machine quietly humming in the far right corner. I had never seen it before, but intuitively, I knew exactly what it was.

The altering machine.

The devious invention Paul used to change me into the perfect image of his dream girl, and turn my own dream of beauty into a nightmare.

My body shook slightly as I stared at it, and like a moth to a deadly flame, I took a drawn and captivated step forward. The smooth black metal of the machine had one brilliant shine down the middle from the ceiling lights, and despite its plain appearance, the allure of its power fascinated me. I could hardly believe something man-made could erase and recreate an entire life, yet I had been a victim of its rare, unequaled curse.

I stopped just a few inches in front of it, compelled to touch the surface with my fingertips before I started to search for the Bioim powder.

But—

"*Dana!*"

Paul's voice erupted through the basement from the top of the staircase. I spun around, my heart pounding with more force than what seemed possible as the air in my lungs constricted. A tense moment of silence passed before Paul's feet rapidly struck each step while he made his way down, and only a few seconds later, he stood in the open doorway.

I anxiously stepped back against the machine while our eyes locked, hoping to endure nothing worse than his emotional temper. Paul wore a wrinkled white tank top and green fleece bottoms that made me think he had just rolled out of bed, but I couldn't imagine what mistake had ruined my plan.

"What are you doing down here?" he snapped.

My lungs slowly expanded as my initial shock faded, and before I spoke, I already felt any answer—whether it be true or a lie—would be useless to calm him.

"I—I wanted to see the m-machine that changed me," I replied. "I got up for a glass of water, and then..."

Paul's eyes narrowed and stared at me darkly through his glasses, the red tinge of anger in his face remaining.

"You got up for water, Dana?"

"Yes. I tried to be quiet, and I didn't mean to come down into—"

"Shut up. You're lying."

My eyes widened as I fell into a mental spiral of confusion, unable to explain his presence or what he knew of my true intentions.

"Paul, I'm not..."

"Why are you dressed, then? It's obvious I'm not handsome, but *you* should be well aware of how smart I am. In fact, you should know I have more intelligence than you ever will, and it's clear that you're down here to find the powder before you leave me."

Tears of stress stung at the corners of my eyes as I failed to think of how I could deny it. My weak lies were all I had to possibly defend my actions and turn the situation around, but Paul had too easily seen through them, and I could tell forgiveness would not be readily given.

"How did you know I was down here?" I asked, though hardly above a whisper.

"A camera," Paul said after a moment. "Your room was empty."

My mouth fell open while a new dose of horror and fear surged through me. Of course, I was being watched. I felt like I should have known it all along—that I could never have an ounce of privacy within the walls of his house. But I didn't get a chance to respond before Paul moved toward me. My body felt paralyzed as he made a slight turn to the wooden counter that ran along the back wall. He grabbed a square tin box from a shelf above the counter, then opened the lid.

What's in...?

My heart pounded as I saw him immediately lift a syringe from the box, the plunger sticking out far as if it were already full. I hardly stared a few seconds at it before every atom of my being screamed for me to run.

I bolted for the door and made it through the main room of the basement, but when I reached the staircase, Paul was already a few feet behind me. I scrambled up the steps toward the door, but his hand caught my left foot halfway up, and I fell into the stairs, hitting my forehead on the edge of the wooden step.

I cried out in pain, forcing myself to ignore the throb in my head as I flipped to my back. Paul stood above me with the syringe in his hand, his eyes impossible to see through the glare of light across his glasses. A small smile turned the corner of his mouth as he raised the syringe in the air—as if preparing to sink the needle into me with all his might. I stared in horror while I wondered if my new life, just like my old one, would end forever now. Although I didn't know what he had in the syringe, I knew it would make me totally helpless and finally enslaved to him and his pheromone if I didn't find a way to escape.

Paul suddenly dropped forward and held his body above mine, causing a burst of firy determination to surge through me. My knee collided hard with his stomach just before the needle pierced the side of my neck, and I shoved him sideways into the wall, freed from being pinned beneath him. I flipped back to my stomach and lunged to the top of the staircase, hearing Paul huffing and groaning angrily behind me.

The front door felt unreachable during the few seconds of eternity it took me to sprint to it. Without hesitation, I turned the deadbolt just as I heard Paul's footsteps strike the floor hastily behind me. The front door swung open and I raced into the thick darkness outside, my desperate speed fueled by unrestrained adrenaline. Paul screamed my name repeatedly as the gravel crunched beneath my feet, but when I reached the forest edge across the road, I vanished into the night—fleeing into a maze of pines like the rest of my life depended on it.

5 - MENTAL

Bright sunrays poured through the window of my hospital room the next day. I lay in the middle of the bed with pillows tucked behind my back, trying to distract myself with something on the mounted TV. Although I felt certain Paul knew nothing of my whereabouts or that he could even do anything to me here, I still shivered at the thought of him roaming the halls to find and drag me back to his basement.

As I ran through the dark, shadowed forest last night, I felt convinced Paul was right behind me several times, though I never truly knew. And how far he had pursued me from his house I couldn't tell, but eventually I came upon another paved road, where a kind stranger pulled over and agreed to take me to the hospital. It all seemed like a fever dream while I tried to relax in my safe new surroundings, but despite no sleep after checking in around midnight, I still felt wide awake.

My nurse had called the police station for me that morning, and when Detective Shaw entered my private room a short while later, I finally started to feel better. He had black hair and looked to be in his mid-thirties, and wore a blue button up shirt and black slacks. The detective carried a leather portfolio with a legal pad inside, and I smiled politely while he grabbed a chair and brought it to my bedside.

"Good morning. I'm Detective Rob Shaw, as you may know. I spoke to your nurse Abby earlier," he said as he sat down. "How are you feeling?"

"I'm alright, thank you."

"Abby told me you were dropped off here last night after you escaped someone who was holding you captive. Were you kidnapped?"

"Yes."

"Were you assaulted in any way?"

"No, not exactly. I hit my head on a staircase when I was trying to get away from him, but he did something else…"

"What?"

"He… he changed how I look entirely."

Detective Shaw furrowed his eyebrows and opened the leather portfolio, quickly scribbling some notes on the yellow paper. My whole body tensed as I realized how impossible the truth would sound, but it was too important to hide—no matter how crazy it seemed.

"He changed how you look?"

"Yes, and you probably won't believe it, but I'm..."

"Dana Carter? Your nurse said you gave that name when you checked in."

I nodded, biting my bottom lip.

"Why do you claim to be her? There is a Dana Carter that's been missing from this area for several days, but the two of you could not look more different."

My gaze fell to my lap and I sighed heavily, balling my hands into loose fists.

"I know, but like I said, he changed my appearance entirely. I promise I'm Dana Carter—I have no reason to lie. The man who kidnapped me is a terrible genius who developed a machine that can do things to people no one else knows about yet."

"What is his name?"

"Paul Henderson."

"How did he kidnap you?"

"I wrecked my car a few nights ago and he took me from the crash while I was blacked out, but I think he might have caused it."

"What is his house address?"

After I said it, Detective Shaw wrote it down on his legal pad, but he took another minute to scribble more notes.

"How exactly do you believe he changed your physical appearance?" he asked calmly.

"There's a machine in his basement that he put me in, and I don't know exactly how it works because I woke up from the accident looking like this. And I know it sounds crazy, but you have to believe me. If you search his house you'll find everything—including my belongings, things that belong to Dana Carter."

Detective Shaw nodded and looked away thoughtfully, leaving me in painful anticipation of what he might decide.

"I can only obtain a search warrant if I have probable cause of a crime," he said at length. "The body-altering machine you described isn't going to hold merit with a judge, but if I request a warrant to secure evidence of your kidnapping, that will very likely be granted."

"Of course—whatever you have to do."

The detective nodded, then sighed in a way that made me feel uneasy.

"It will be easier for me to help you if I know who you really are," he said gently. "Are you trying to assume another identity to feel safe or leave your life behind?"

I blinked, shaking my head.

"No. I *am* Dana Carter and what I said happened is true. You'll understand when you see the machine."

"Have you ever gone by another name?"

"No, never. But Paul also admitted that he killed a man named Jordan Stoll years ago—someone he went to college with. He has the article of his death on the wall of his basement, along with the portrait of a woman who is also dead. You have to get the warrant as soon as possible and arrest him!"

I didn't mean to raise my voice, but the depth of Paul's sinister acts quickly shook my core. Detective Shaw wrote for a few minutes before he finally closed the leather portfolio and stood.

"You should get some rest, now," he insisted. "I'll be in touch about the warrant and any charges."

I smiled and he promptly left, but instead of feeling a whole lot better, I felt stuck in a web of crimes too incredulous and murky to be solved.

● ● ● ● ● ●

My nurse Abby returned that evening with a tray of food—the smell of which caused my mouth to suddenly water. After she placed it on a table that hovered above my lap on a stand, I quickly took bites of the chicken breast, broccoli and macaroni.

"I can imagine you're starving," she remarked. "When was the last time you ate something?"

I shrugged, not even trying to remember.

"Did Shaw tell you anything?" I asked.

"Yes," she replied, a bit stiffly.

"I know what I told him must seem crazy, but once he gets the warrant, it will all make sense. Paul is a mad genius who can do incredible but really terrible things with that machine."

Abby nodded as I continued to eat, her expression filled with polite but doubtful understanding. I frowned and looked away, hiding my disappointment that she didn't believe the truth anymore than the detective.

"Detective Shaw actually spoke with me and your doctor not long ago on the phone, and we think it would be very helpful for you to spend the next few weeks at the Mulden-Hale center," she said pleasantly at length. "Your mental health is just as important as anything else after all you have been through."

Although hope and encouragement filled her tone, my heart quickly sank at the true meaning of her words.

"I'm being sent to a psychiatric hospital?"

"It's not permanent," she assured quickly. "But the doctor believes there may be trauma you need to work through to remember who you are or to accept it and move forward. Detective Shaw told us how convinced you are about being Dana Carter, and we think the best doctors at Mulden-Hale should work with you on that."

I stopped chewing the piece of chicken in my mouth as my gaze fell from her to my almost empty dinner plate. My heart thudded loudly in my ears as I tried to rationalize the surprising decision each of them had made without my consent, and without even looking into any of my claims—no matter how improbable.

"I can't go to Mulden-Hale," I said firmly. "It makes no sense before the search warrant, because they'll find the machine and see what Paul did to me. But ask me anything about my—Dana Carter's life, and I can tell you anything you want to know. Please Abby, I'm not lying!"

Tears slid across my cheeks unexpectedly as my temperature rose and the muscles in my back ached from painful tension. The nurse put her hand on my arm and started rubbing my shoulder in deep circular motions.

"You are going to be just fine," she insisted gently. "Detective Shaw will do all that he can to make sure everything is taken care of."

"I need to talk to him. I'm not going to Mulden-Hale until he gets the search warrant, which he said he would do to look into my kidnapping. You can disbelieve whatever I say about who I am, but I *was* taken against my will!"

"Okay, you can talk to him tomorrow. But you need to focus on calming down and getting decent sleep tonight."

I sighed heavily and leaned back into the bed pillows, my cheeks streaked with tears I didn't bother to wipe away while I stared at the ceiling.

I'm not setting foot inside a mental hospital until every inch of Paul's property is searched—I'm not the crazy one.

"If you need anything, just press this button on the side of your bed," Abby said, guiding my hand to a small red button. "My shift is over in a half hour, but another nurse will be available to help. Please try not to overwhelm yourself tonight, okay?"

I nodded once, though I kept my eyes on the ceiling. Abby sighed and slowly turned from me, then walked to the door and exited. My mind spun while I squeezed my eyes shut, remembering my chance for justice and vindication had a timetable no one knew about.

Because I no longer had access to Bioim powder, the time I had left was extremely limited. And as much as I wanted to believe it was nothing but a lie for his control... I had no good reason to doubt it, especially after what he had already done to me.

And Becky and Jordan.

If Shaw can't or won't get me the justice I deserve very soon... I'll go back to Paul's house, and I'll do it myself.

6 - RUN

Abby walked me to the nurses station early the next afternoon so I could call Detective Shaw. After he confirmed his intention to get the warrant for my kidnapping, I begged Abby to let me stay at the hospital until Paul's property had been searched.

"Please tell the doctor that Shaw is going to have the search done this week," I insisted. "I shouldn't go to Mulden-Hale before they've had a chance to find any proof of what I'm saying. It's all there in the basement."

"Okay, I will talk to her about it," Abby replied. "I'm sure we can keep you here at least another week."

I grinned at her as I stepped into my room alone, and when Abby closed the door, I waited a minute before pulling out a brochure of the hospital from beneath my bed mattress. I noticed the edge of it sticking out from under the bed after I showered that morning, and it restored a lot of hope I had been lacking. I climbed on my bed and sat with my legs crossed before I opened the first flap, which had a map of the first and second levels. But the center section had the third and fourth levels—the latter being my location.

I need to know my way around this place, because if something goes wrong and I ever set foot inside Mulden-Hale...

A chill raced down my spine as I saw myself confined to a room inside that mental hospital, dying alone and without justice, or even a name.

● ● ● ● ● ●

Four days later, Abby led me into a private office to receive an update from Detective Shaw. He had managed to get the search warrant a day after our last conversation, and I could hardly wait to hear about the raid of Paul's basement, as well as the investigation into the horrific altering machine.

After Abby left the room, I picked up the desk phone and took the detective off hold, hoping to hear that Paul was currently sitting somewhere charged in handcuffs.

Before I spoke, I took a deep breath.

"Detective Rob Shaw? It's me—Dana."

"Yes, well, hello. I want to give you an update on the search my team and I conducted yesterday of Paul Henderson's residence. Unfortunately we were not able to find any of the items you said would be there, but we did inspect the machine—which looked exactly as you described—in the basement. It's not functioning and did not appear to have any ability to generate radiation. Paul told us it's an old oxygen chamber he bought years ago as a novelty interest. Whether that's true or not, we have no way to prove at this time."

I hardly saw the hallway in front of me as my hopes and heart sank with every word.

What did he do after I escaped? None of this makes any sense!

Despite blinking a few times, it didn't seem possible for me to break free of my stunned trance, which had blocked out the entire world around me.

"I—I can't believe this," I said, my voice shaking. "He must have gotten rid of my belongings, because he took them from the car wreck and kept my journal for himself. Did you search all the rooms, the garage, any sheds—?"

"Yes, we searched it all thoroughly and could find nothing that tied him to you, or anything suspicious for that matter. I'm sorry."

"He must have gotten rid of my stuff then! And he lied about the machine—it's not an oxygen chamber. I don't know how it works because I was unconscious inside it, but Paul told me he used it to alter my DNA and change how I look. Please, I'm *not* crazy. What about the article of Jordan Stoll's death? Or Becky's portrait? Did you see that?"

There was a short pause on Detective Shaw's end until he sighed heavily.

"No... neither of those things were uncovered. We did confirm that Paul and Jordan attended Strathsmith together and that Jordan died his senior year from a collision with another vehicle, but police reports of the incident said Jordan was driving too fast and did not obey the stop sign at the intersection, which ultimately led to the wreck and his death."

"Well that isn't all there is to it," I protested. "Paul admitted to tampering with his brakes like I told you. Jordan probably couldn't stop his car which is why he hit the other vehicle."

"If that is true, it would be too late to investigate now. Insurance records with the police report say the vehicle was junked because it was totaled."

I bit my lip hard to try to focus and stop my head from spinning. No matter what I said or how murderous and deranged I knew Paul to be, every effort I could use to expose him had failed.

Except one, maybe.

"How does he say we met if he didn't take me from my car wreck?" I asked defensively. "How can he explain me being at his house and knowing about the machine? My hair and fingerprints must be all over the place."

Detective Shaw cleared his throat in a way that sounded uneasy.

"Paul claims that you knocked on his door one night in distress, and he let you in to use the phone," he replied. "He said he heard you call your family and tell them you would never see them again, and that you told him you were Dana Carter afterward."

My mouth fell open as I gasped, horrified.

"*What?* That's not true at all!"

"He then claimed you left later that night after he caught you going through his belongings upstairs and in the basement. I know how strongly you believe the things you've told me and I don't want to upset you, but Paul's story is easier to believe and corroborate in regards to your interactions with each other."

My blood raced as I felt myself begin to slip down an intense and familiar dark spiral. Somehow, Paul had cleverly managed to deflect every terrible truth about himself... which finally left me as the crazy, nameless woman those who had a chance of helping me already suspected and wanted to believe.

"Who did you call at his house?" Detective Shaw asked. "You may be suffering from some type of amnesia or dissociative identity disorder. Whoever you called may have more answers about you or this case."

I squeezed my eyes shut to stop any stinging tears from slipping out, but a few fell down my cheeks anyway.

"I called my mom and dad—Mr. and Mrs. Carter."

Within seconds, I slammed the phone down on the receiver. My hope for lawful justice—as hard as I tried—was gone.

● ● ● ● ● ●

My nerves felt on edge the next morning while I ate breakfast after Abby left my room. Because of how upset I felt yesterday, I hadn't told her the details of my phone call with Detective Shaw—though I guessed I didn't need to.

My reaction made the result of our conversation painfully obvious, and I knew either she or my doctor would be filled in soon enough.

I have to get out of here before they take me away to the psych hospital... but when?

Although the urge to leave at some point that morning flooded me, the possibility of being caught caused my blood to race—as well as imagining the moment I finally saw my parents again face to face, but in *this* body.

I pushed the bed table away and closed my eyes, picturing the easiest escape route which took me down an elevator and through the main lobby and cafeteria to an exit door. The simple plan would likely help me leave without much notice... but I still needed to muster the courage.

Should I go now? But why not? I can't drag this out if I don't know how much time I have...

I opened my eyes and sighed heavily.

Although I was scared, I knew I was ready.

I climbed off the bed and grabbed the folded black sweats and white t-shirt Abby had given me a few days ago for my workouts. I slipped them on after removing my hospital gown and approached the door, peeking through a small gap into the hallway. Two nurses and a doctor chatted while walking toward me, and I quickly pulled the door closed until they passed.

When I stepped into the hallway, I moved briskly toward the nurses station, though a woman in casual business attire sat in a chair with her back to me. She had a binder and stack of folders in her lap that kept her attention, and my gaze stayed fixed on her until I made it to the elevators.

I immediately pressed the downward arrow and glanced at the woman again—who I assumed was an admin—but she was still preoccupied.

What would she think of me anyway? She doesn't know I'm the infamous Jane Doe here... right?

I pressed the button again impatiently, trying not to think about what might happen if Abby spotted me. When the elevator to my left finally opened, I sighed in relief as I stepped into the large, empty space. The button for the lobby lit up as I pushed it with my finger, and I felt a strong sense of accomplishment once the elevator doors slid closed.

That wasn't too bad... maybe I can get out of here easily. But what if the cafeteria is full? Or what if it isn't?

I weighed the pros and cons until the elevator finally stopped. I blinked as the doors immediately opened, though my gaze dropped when a man and woman—dressed normally like visitors—stepped in as I walked out. The crowded ground-floor lobby was noisy while I made my way across it toward the cafeteria, which looked even larger than the lobby through its floor to ceiling glass walls.

I soon passed into the dining area after pulling open one of its shiny silver doors, and I blended into the countless people around me who wore normal clothes, though some had scrubs. A red exit sign into the courtyard on the right side of the building caught my attention, and I quickly started weaving my way between people toward it.

Almost there! Just got to get through that door, into the courtyard and through a small patch of trees, then—

"Hey! What are you doing?"

My heart skipped a beat as I felt a hand suddenly lock around my wrist and abruptly stop me. My gaze widened as I stared at a man in navy scrubs to my left, who stared back with furrowed eyebrows.

"What are you doing down here?" he asked suspiciously. "I've seen you. You're our Jane Doe from the fourth floor."

I hardly knew what to say while being overwhelmed with shock, but finally I managed to recover just enough.

"I—um—I need some air."

"Air?"

"My nurse, she—Abby gave me permission."

"We don't give patients permission to freely walk the hospital or go outside for air. You need to go back up to your room."

The tall man started to pull me toward one of the cafeteria doors, but a frightened scream escaped my throat, startling me as I jerked my wrist free of his hold. The man looked at me in surprise for a split second before I turned, desperately running through the tables and groups of people to reach the exit door.

"Stop!"

With every step, I imagined his firm grip upon my shoulder, stopping me before I could reach the courtyard door. But within minutes, I fled into fresh air and bright sunlight, hoping I could make it off the property before security caught me.

7 - HOME

I walked into a convenience store and called a cab less than a half hour after making a break from the hospital. When the driver arrived, I hardly said a word as I climbed into the backseat, preferring to stare out the window silently while I tried to stay calm.

I didn't have any money to pay him, yet—but he didn't need to know that. All he needed to do was to finally take me *home*.

I don't care if I die soon. But it must be with the only people in the only place that make me feel safe and happy now...

The beautiful white house my parents lived in on ten acres of land sat almost twenty miles from the hospital, and for most of the drive, I relived my happiest memories there, most of which were birthdays, sleepovers, late night talks on the porch, outdoor explorations, and finding my first car in the driveway with a bow on the hood...

I swallowed hard and looked down at my perfectly slender hands with naturally shiny nails.

Not one moment of this body is worth what I've been through...

When the cab turned onto Fulton Road ten minutes later, I abandoned my dark mental spiral and sat straighter as I stared out the windshield. My family home soon appeared further down the dirt road, and I grinned while staring at my mom's red SUV parked in the gravel driveway beside the house.

The cab driver turned into the winding driveway a few minutes later and eventually parked behind the SUV. My heart pounded while I numbly grasped the door handle and told him to wait for me to get the money I owed. Once I stepped out of the cab, I slowly walked toward the wide front porch, then climbed the steps to the front door. My nerves hardly felt the metal screen door as I pulled it open, knocking lightly on the main door behind it.

Maybe she won't hear me, but I'm too terrified to knock any harder...

I waited a minute before I raised my hand again, but this time, just as my knuckles nearly touched the front door—it opened.

I hardly knew what to do as my mother and I suddenly stared at each other in tense silence full of surprise and awkwardness. She wore a blue blouse and white pants on her short, rounded frame—a type of body we both used to share.

"Hi, honey," she said, her tone soft but concerned. "Can I help you?"

I blinked, then smiled a little.

"Um, yes... you can. I have information about Dana Carter."

Her eyes widened as her face became riddled with shock.

"What? Are you serious?"

"Yes, but I need to pay the cab that brought me here. If you go into... Dana's room, you'll find a twenty dollar bill in the top drawer of her desk. It's under the yellow notepad."

The surprise on my mother's face broadened before she finally turned away. I watched as she disappeared around the left corner of the entry hall, though she came back less than ten seconds later. My brow furrowed as she held out a twenty dollar bill to me, which I suspected had come from her purse that she liked to keep in the kitchen and not my bedroom at all.

I took the money anyway and walked back to the cab, then returned to my mother. She stepped aside to let me in, and the bright daylight that filled the entry hall vanished when she closed the door behind me.

"How do you know my daughter?" she asked immediately.

I inhaled deeply and dropped my gaze to the floor, having no idea of where to begin.

"Do you mind if we sit down? It's not easy what I have to tell you."

My mother nodded once and I followed her to the end of the entry hall into the living room. The wide space had a large couch and two recliners that faced a TV and fireplace. Most of the kitchen could easily be seen on the right side of the room, and a sliding glass door beside the breakfast table led out to the back deck.

My mother sat stiffly in the maroon recliner near the left end of the couch, and I settled into the far right couch cushion—my favorite spot in the living room since my parents had bought the couch a few years ago. Although I wanted to draw up my legs and wrap my arms around them, I resisted making myself too comfortable in my own home—yet.

I smiled a little uncomfortably while my mother stared in anticipation, for I almost dreaded having to explain the truth now.

What if she rejects me and thinks I'm crazy too?

I swallowed hard and took a breath.

"I just spent several days in the hospital after I was held captive by a man named Paul, who took me from a car accident," I said slowly. "I had been driving back to my dorm from an honors retreat at Lake Tahoe, but it was raining and I saw deer and I—"

Tears stung at my eyes as I paused for a second.

"I crashed in a deep ditch. My car was a beautiful blue-gray civic I got for my birthday a few years ago. I promise I'm not trying to lie or trick you, but I'm—I'm—"

My mother covered her mouth with her hand as I dropped my gaze and wiped my cheeks. My heart pounded as I waited for her to realize I had hinted at my true identity, but I hardly had any patience.

"I know it will seem impossible, but I'm Dana, mom. The man who took me from the accident changed my whole body."

My mother gasped as her hand fell away from her mouth, and she shook her head quickly.

"I can't imagine what you've been through, honey, but you're not Dana—"

My hands became fists in my lap as desperation overtook me, and I glanced at the large family photo collage above the fireplace.

"That picture of me, you, and dad on the beach was taken during our Florida vacation nine years ago. I remember you being really stressed because I wouldn't stay still and it was windy, then dad got a phone call that kept him busy for twenty minutes. But eventually, we got the perfect shot. That other picture is of my kindergarten graduation, and the one next to it is one of my horseback riding lessons before I went to college."

I watched as her eyes widened and her mouth fell open slightly, but I couldn't stop yet—not until I was *positive* she believed me.

"You love the shower curtain in your bathroom because the flowers on it remind you of your wedding bouquet. The blue quilt on the end of my bed was made by Grandma Helen before she died, and there's a big stain on the basement carpet from when I spilled one of my paint sets as a kid."

While I spoke, the surprise on my mother's face grew, until she wore an expression full of emotions that I couldn't easily read.

"You can't be her... but you know things... things someone wouldn't even think to ask..."

Her voice was breathy and full of disbelief, though I knew my memories were starting to convince her.

"Ever since I went to college, I hated how I looked more than I ever had before," I said, my voice shaking as more tears rolled along my cheeks. "I kept a secret diary about it, and when Paul kidnapped me, he read it and put me inside a machine that changed how I look—but he had his own reasons, too. I don't care if you believe that, though, mom. I just need you to believe that I'm your daughter, Dana."

A few more tears slid down my cheeks while stress and desperation caused my muscles to tense. But I managed to feel some relief when my mother left the recliner and sat down a few inches from me, her hands resting on top of my shoulders.

"Who was your best friend in ninth grade?"

"Elizabeth Newton."

"And what almost ended your friendship?"

"She moved to Connecticut right after sophomore year."

My mother made a joyful sound as she pulled me into a tight hug. I grinned as I finally began to relax, savoring her warm and safe embrace.

"You look like a model from a magazine," she confessed. "But it has to be you—I know it's you, Dana. Maybe I'll never understand how, but I know it's you."

Despite every fear and the odds against me, my life and home had been reclaimed.

8 - BURN

The week following my return home turned into the best of my life. Paul and my impending death faded into the back of my mind as I lived like I never had before: truly satisfied with each of my blessings, and finally at peace with what I saw in the mirror—though beauty had nothing to do with it now.

A new sense of wholeness I had never felt from life itself reflected in my eyes, and I knew I didn't need an entire lifetime to soak it in fully.

Already, I was thoroughly saturated.

My father also realized the truth of my identity after I shared my memories with him when he returned home a few hours after I spoke to my mother the first day. And despite a few passing fears, no one from the hospital or police department ever came knocking on our door—though I supposed it made sense in some way.

I wasn't a criminal after all.

Just a formerly lost, nameless girl.

Despite five nights of the deepest, most peaceful sleep I could remember, I lay awake one night while staring at the shadows of trees and bright wedges of moonlight on the ceiling. The large gas can I noticed in the garage that day kept me awake, for I imagined pouring trails of the golden liquid inside a certain log cabin, then setting it ablaze.

I could burn everything he has to the ground... and he can go with it.

My pulse quickened as I closed my eyes and inhaled deeply. The keys to my parents cars hung on the wall beside the garage door, which made my impulsively formed plan to grab the gas can and drive to Paul's house practically effortless...

He's probably in the basement right now and wouldn't notice the fire until it was too late—until it was burning all around him. But I can't really do this... can I?

I stared at the ceiling a while longer before I slowly sat up, trying to build the nerve to put my desire in motion.

Because of him, I'll be dead soon. And the police will never know... nothing will ever be done about it.

I climbed off my bed and changed out of an oversized t-shirt into a hoodie and jeans before quietly leaving my room. The dark house was perfectly silent while I carefully made my way to the kitchen, where I grabbed my mother's car keys and slipped into the garage. After flipping the light switch, I saw the red gas can on the opposite side of the open space, sitting on a wooden countertop beneath a single window.

I passed the front of my parent's vehicles to grab it, though my heart nearly skipped a beat when I saw two wonderful match boxes resting beside the gas can.

If I ever needed a sign, this is it!

I grabbed the gas and the matches, then walked to the driver's door of my mother's SUV. Inside, I put the gas and matches on the passenger seat before settling in and pressing the garage door opener. The long sheet of metal lifted more quietly than I expected, and I backed into the driveway a minute later.

My nerves finally caught up to me once I drove along the empty road, leaving the safety of my home behind in the dark, quiet night. Although my breathing spiked as I felt the urge to turn back, I kept driving straight ahead—forcing myself through fear to claim whatever justice I could.

Keep going... it won't take long.

While I drove, I wondered how long it would take Paul's house to turn to ash, for I knew a fire *could* consume a house within minutes.

Hopefully, I would be so lucky.

I made it through town in twenty minutes and turned onto another long, empty road made of dirt. This one led out of Carson City toward Lake Tahoe, though I wouldn't have to go nearly that far before I reached Paul's house. Because of my many trips into town, I knew exactly how to get there, but I felt a chill run down my spine at the thought of setting foot on his property once again.

Even if he isn't there, I'm still burning his house to the ground. There's no turning back when I leave once and for all...

The number of pine trees increased the farther I drove, and eventually, I started slowing down when I sensed Paul's house drawing closer. It sat on top of a high slope of land I had gradually been climbing, and I hit the brakes a minute later when I spotted his mailbox and yellow outdoor house lights. I stared briefly at the ominous cabin before I put the SUV in reverse and parked it alongside the road, several yards from Paul's driveway. As my heart pounded, I tried not to think about what I was doing when I grabbed the gas can and matches, then left the SUV.

The warm night air felt sticky while I walked in the darkness toward his house, hoping no other vehicles would pass and catch me in their headlights. But I made it to the driveway without notice, and again stared at the house in awe—hardly able to believe what impossible changes happened there.

I sighed heavily and started walking; my gaze darting to each bright window in case Paul suddenly appeared behind one of them. When I got close to the garage, I saw his truck parked inside through a long, narrow window in the garage door. Although the outdoor lights and glowing windows suggested his presence, his truck became the final confirmation.

I briskly walked toward the right side of the house and ducked beneath the first window, but stopped under the second one, which belonged to my old room. After setting the gas can and matches in the grass, I carefully rose up in front of the dark glass, grateful to find the room empty.

This is it... my way in. I hope Paul didn't lock the window after I left.

I grasped the window frame and gently pushed upward, suddenly relieved that it lifted easily without a sound. But my victory was short-lived when an obvious, yet delayed thought crossed my mind—*where is Paul?*

I left the window open as I sunk to the ground, realizing I needed to circle the cabin and figure out his location before sneaking in. I crept along the side of the house and turned the corner, keeping myself hunched beneath the bright, uncovered windows facing the backyard.

The largest window in the middle would help me see into the dining room, kitchen, and living room at once, so I slowly crept beneath it, taking a few seconds to ready myself before I looked.

When my gaze fell through the bright glass, I glanced into each of the three rooms—thankful not to spot Paul in any of them, or any clear sign he was around. I quickly ducked beneath the window again, convinced that he almost certainly had to be in the basement, which had no windows.

Where else would he be but down there?

I waited another minute before stealing a second look into the house; this time catching a glimpse of the basement door, which stood ajar.

Maybe that's a sign? There's nothing else I can do...

My heart thudded in my ears while I made my way back to the window of my old room. After lifting the window all the way, I grabbed the gas can and set it against the left side of the window pane. I then tucked the matchboxes in my pocket and began to climb in, flexing the top half of my body uncomfortably through the square gap. When I started falling toward the floor, I stretched out my arms to catch myself, and slowly crawled forward until I pulled my legs in far enough and my feet dropped behind me—though not as quietly as I would have liked.

Like a defenseless animal, I listened for any sounds of my predator, but the silence within the house went unbroken as the minutes passed.

I sighed and stood, grabbing the gas can from the window pane and approaching the bedroom door as quietly as I could.

The door opened easily without a sound, and I passed from the bedroom into the hall, still alert for any reason to turn back and escape. But the silence continued as I cautiously walked toward the living room at the end of the dark hall, my mind filling with memories of the dance Paul made me share with him there, as well as a forced kiss.

A shiver ran down my spine while I suddenly considered the terror my life might have truly had if he managed to brainwash me with the pheromone before I ran—yet another devious invention I believed he would eventually figure out, just like the machine.

I passed from hallway shadows into the living room that was lit by a few lamps and drifting light from the kitchen and dining room. Again, I paused to listen to the silence and make sure it went uninterrupted, though part of me wished I could hear Paul in the basement to easily keep track of him.

I sighed and shook my head, trying to focus on my moment of justice, which had *finally* come.

Time to burn this place of nightmares to the ground...

I pulled the plug from the gas can spout as I walked toward the couch, dumping the golden liquid along the top and across the cushions. I then soaked the drapes behind the couch and TV within a few minutes, and poured what was left of the gasoline on the wide rug under the coffee table. I pulled the matches from my pocket after setting down the gas can and struck one against the side of the box, watching the red head ignite into flame. I tossed it onto the couch and another lit match onto the rug—both of which were immediately consumed in fire.

I turned from the living room and sprinted back into the bedroom, exiting the window rapidly and falling onto the grass without catching myself. I hardly noticed the painful throb in my left wrist and shoulder as I jumped to my feet and fled into the pine trees. The same horror from the night Paul chased me fueled my adrenaline, but before I got too far away, I suddenly stopped and caught my breath.

Paul wouldn't find me, and more than anything, I wanted to see his house burn.

Despite my urge to return to my mother's SUV, I turned back and retraced my steps far enough to see the edge of the treeline. I walked away from the side of the house and stopped only when I reached the darkness of the trees that faced the back of his house. Through the windows, I could see the drapes falling apart while flames ate at them, and more patches of fire blazed throughout the house.

As to where Paul was or what he knew of the danger... I didn't care.

"Now we can die together."

The words left my mouth bleakly, and from the corner of my eye, I spotted an object that faintly reflected the intensifying light from the house.

My gaze narrowed as I tried to make sense of it, but once I took a few steps closer, I gasped as my hand fell across my lips. A large, polished white stone laid flat on the ground in freshly disturbed dirt, as if it had been recently placed or returned, or both.

In the middle of its rectangular shape, a few words were carved imperfectly, as though etched by hand upon a tombstone:

BECKY HENDERSON

MY FIRST BELOVED

DARK TRUTH

JEREMY

1 - GONE

The month of August became the worst time of year for my family and I ten years ago. My nine year old little brother, Oliver, disappeared on August twenty-ninth during a camping trip, and despite an investigation, there hadn't been a trace of him since—though I supposed that is how it usually went with the people who vanished suddenly into thin air.

Of course, no one in the immediate Gregory family had been the same since, and after two years, we decided to gather every August twenty-ninth to honor his memory—just like we did for his birthday soon after in September. After all, neither day was one any of us wanted to spend alone, anyhow.

The gray sky above my parents' street looked gloomy as I drove slowly toward their house close to the end of the block. They lived in a neighborhood full of large craftsman style houses, and their blue house with white trim was where my siblings and I had grown up.

When I turned into their driveway, I parked behind my older sister's silver SUV and climbed out of my small sedan. I walked between it and the red SUV my aunt and uncle owned, for they also chose to celebrate Oliver's life with us twice a year.

My mood turned more bleak with each step toward the front door, and it waited unlocked as I twisted the knob and stepped inside. The foyer had a staircase and a short hallway that led into the kitchen, but it also had an archway into the main living room. I heard my mother and aunt's voices while I slipped off my jacket and hung it on the coat rack, then untied my boots. My mother sounded upset as she spoke, but it was nothing unusual for today.

Even ten years later, Oliver's disappearance still brought her to tears, though it seemed natural that it always would.

I sighed heavily and glanced in the mirror on the wall above a small table and vase of white lilies. My brown hair still looked combed but was a little overgrown, and slight dark wedges lay beneath my gray eyes, standing out a little from my pale, flushed skin.

I forced a small smile on my face and left the foyer for the living room. There, I saw my mother and aunt sitting together on a couch, and I sat on the empty one across from them with a coffee table between us. My mother still looked young for a woman in her mid-sixties, though it helped that she kept her hair dyed and shoulder-length, and wore unique, flattering clothes from several boutiques. My aunt, on the other hand, showed her age through many wrinkles and heavy makeup, and her clothes were plain and faded.

She held my mother's hand tightly in her lap as she laughed and told a funny story about Oliver, making my smile a little more pleasant. When my aunt finished, they both focused on me.

"Hi, Jeremy," my mother said, her tone fragile.

"Hi, mom. Good to see you, aunt Joanne," I replied, then raised a brow at her. "I'm not sure I've heard that story before."

My aunt smiled and nodded.

"It just came to me this morning," she said happily. "But the memory is very vivid now. I wonder if Oliver would still be afraid of spiders?"

"I don't know... but I'm sure he wouldn't be exploring the shed again."

My aunt laughed and I smirked, though my humor faded when my gaze slowly drifted to the mantel above the fireplace, which sat lined with pictures of Oliver. He had been a cute boy with freckles, blue eyes, and dark brown hair, and no matter what he was doing in each photo, almost every one showed his gap-toothed smile.

Although I always felt crushed looking at his photos, I loved the one near the end that my mother had taken of him covered in pancake batter. I remembered that morning years ago when we tried to make breakfast together, and Oliver had accidentally spilled the batter all over the kitchen floor. My past fourteen year-old self felt annoyed and upset at his clumsiness, but now, the memory was treasured—just like any other I had with him.

Who would take my little brother from us and ruin his whole life? What kind of sick person does that?

These questions were a few of many that repeated endlessly in my mind since his disappearance, but I knew—with the deepest pain I had even felt—that no answer was likely to ever be found.

It was something we *all* knew, and had to live with day by day.

"I still remember those bad headaches he started having before the camping trip," I said thoughtfully. "I wonder what that was about?"

My mother shrugged, dabbing her eyes with a tissue while my aunt stroked her hand.

"They were probably just allergy related," she replied. "Some people struggle horribly with it. Didn't Luke have that problem?"

"Oh yes, Diane," my aunt replied, her tone dramatic. "Jeremy, your cousin had sinus headaches year-round for a few years at that age, then it stopped for a while but now he's been having them *again*, just not as frequently."

I nodded politely, unable to relate. Even though I had memories of Oliver curling up into a ball on his bed and whimpering from the pain, I decided to drop the subject. It was insignificant, after all, compared to his vanishing... despite my odd curiosity.

* * * * * *

I parked in front of a convenience store on my way home that evening. After I shut off the engine, I climbed out and walked toward the front doors, wanting to pick up a pop, some junk food, and a new razor.

The teen boy behind the cash register smiled at me when I stepped inside, but I ignored him and went to the refrigerated section along the wall. Once I grabbed a pop, I went to a nearby aisle and chose a bag of chips and caramel cubes, then started looking for a razor.

Radio music played at a comfortable level through speakers in the ceiling, and only two other customers seemed to be shopping with me.

When I finally made it to the checkout counter, I waited behind someone else as a man in a blue baseball cap entered the store. The hair on the back of my neck suddenly stood on end as I stared into his thick, black sunglasses—which weren't necessary at seven o'clock. He wore dirty jeans, a black t-shirt and a brown coat, and as I looked away, I tried to convince myself that nothing was wrong.

He was just a little eerie.

After the person in front of me left, I returned the smile from earlier to the teenage cashier, though I just wanted to calm my nerves.

My day felt bad enough already.

Neither of us said a word as he scanned my items, but just as the teen turned his head from the computer screen, his eyes immediately filled with terror.

"S-sir—what are y-you—"

My heart pounded as I noticed his gaze fell slightly past my head, and I shifted slightly before I felt a cold, circular object pressed into the back of my head.

"Give me everything in your register, or I'll blow his brains all over you."

Although I couldn't see who stood behind me, I broke out in a hot sweat as I could only imagine the deep, firm voice belonging to the strange man in black sunglasses, who I never should have ignored.

"I'm—I'm sorry—I need a key, but I don't—"

The teenage boy grabbed the drawer of the cash register as if to show that he couldn't pull it open. A few seconds of tense silence passed, and I waited, hardly ready to die.

"You have thirty seconds or I pull this trigger."

2 - REGRET

My muscles tensed as I felt the urge to turn and slam my fist into the unknown man's face. But the rage-fueled idea died when the cold gun barrel slid from the back of my hair onto the bare skin behind my ear.

Is he really going to kill me over a few hundred dollars?

I swallowed hard, waiting while the cashier muttered nervously and looked around for the key—a key that he obviously didn't have.

But I couldn't die. Not like this.

I took a deep breath.

One... two...

I ducked and spun around, my left fist flying toward the side of the armed robber's face. The man grunted in what seemed like pain and surprise while he stumbled back, and

I charged him, knocking him to the floor as I dove and shoved my shoulder into his stomach. But I hardly had time to lift myself before a shot rang out, and a few people screamed.

I blinked—anticipating a surge of pain to rip through me—but then I saw the gun pointed toward the ceiling, and scrambled to take it from him.

The man kicked me in the chest while I struggled to reach his hand, and just before he pointed the gun at me, I slapped it from his hold. He flipped on his stomach and tried crawling toward it, but by then, another man helped me pin him down.

A crowd started forming while more people entered the store, and soon, the teen cashier announced that he had called the police.

● ● ● ● ● ●

I didn't want to go to work two days later on Monday morning. But somehow—after numbly going through the motions of showering and dressing—I found myself in the parking lot, waiting to climb out of my car.

The week of Oliver's disappearance never seemed like it could get any worse through the years, but after almost losing my life in a robbery attempt at the convenience store, my depression deepened and lingered longer.

The world would be a lot better off if good people knew what bad things were coming... I could have tackled that guy the minute he walked in the store, and someone could have saved Oliver before he was taken...

I pushed open the driver's door and climbed out into the chilly morning air, then made my way toward the front doors of the medical supply building where I worked. Inside the small lobby, the middle-aged receptionist Dawn greeted me, and I nodded once as I passed her, entering a door a few feet from her desk.

The large room on the other side had several offices and groups of cubicles in the middle, and I walked toward my cubicle on the right side of the room. After hanging my jacket off the back of my chair, I sat down in front of the computer, trying to get back a feeling of normalcy as I loaded the CRM program.

"Hey, Jeremy. Good morning."

I immediately looked at the opening of my cubicle, smiling as Julie Carmichael stood there. Her blonde hair was pulled back into a bun, and her blue eyes and red lips stood out from her tanned skin. She wore a white and pink button-up shirt, along with black slacks and heels. Although I dreaded telling her what happened at the convenience store, it almost felt impossible to be down in her presence.

"How was time with your family?"

Her eyebrows furrowed in concern, for she knew I went because of Oliver.

"A mix of good memories and old despair—the usual for us now. But when I went to the store afterward to pick up a few things, I was almost killed during a robbery."

Julie's eyes widened as her mouth fell open slightly.

"What? Are you kidding?"

"No. Some guy tried to rob the store while I was in the checkout line, and he put a gun to my head. But I tackled him to the floor and a few other people helped me hold him down until the cops came."

"Why didn't you call or text me about this?"

"Sorry—I've been talking to my family non-stop about it and haven't had a second to breathe. I was hoping I'd feel better today, and I do a little."

Julie sighed heavily and leaned her shoulder against the cubicle wall.

"I'm so relieved nothing happened to you, Jeremy. I have to get back to my office, but you'll meet me for lunch in the break room at noon, right?"

I smiled at her play of innocence, because we both knew I wouldn't refuse.

"Of course."

• • • • • •

Julie sat waiting for me at the far end of the long brown table in the break room when I entered a few minutes past twelve. She waved at me and I nodded, quickly eyeing her sandwich, chips, yogurt and granola bar in front of her near a gray lunch bag.

My lunch—a cheap microwave meal—had been unceremoniously tossed in a plastic bag that morning, and I threw the bag out once I grabbed the meal box and set it on the counter. After I prepped it and put it in the microwave, I turned to Julie, who stared at me with fascination.

"You're a hero," she said, her tone lively. "I found an article about the attempted robbery, and I still can't believe that it happened. Not many people have the courage to fight their attackers—especially when they have a gun. What made you do it?"

"I don't know... I just didn't want to die like that," I replied thoughtfully. "But I've seen a lot of fights in action movies, so maybe something clicked."

"Maybe," she said with a laugh. "Or maybe you should quit customer service and become a bodyguard."

"Yeah, right. I mean, I totally smoked that guy, but I'm not sure I could do it again."

The microwave dinged and I turned, popping open the door and taking the meal box out. After I grabbed a plastic fork and a few napkins, I sat in an empty chair next to Julie.

"Before I walked in this morning, I was thinking... wouldn't it be great if there was some way to know about bad things before they happened?"

I took a bite of my lava-hot macaroni while Julie nodded and pulled a spoon clean of yogurt from between her lips.

"Of course it would be. Everyone wants that."

"What's the best way, though? Visions, mind-reading, or something else?"

"Visions could be very handy, but it might cause havoc if people randomly stopped what they were doing all the time to witness one."

"Sure—unless you got the visions at night, like a dream or something."

"That could work."

"What about mind-reading? I kind of think it would be less efficient because there might not always be enough time to stop someone before they do something terrible—but I guess a lot of bad things are planned, so, maybe it would still help."

Julie shrugged, her gaze falling into her yogurt container.

"I think humanity as a whole would prefer visions, because—do you really want someone reading your thoughts all day? At least visions are selective about what you see and know."

"That makes sense. What are you hiding, Julie?"

I smirked and gently pinched her arm, causing her to gasp and smack my hand away.

"There's something you should see in the warehouse," she said after a moment. "Do you have time to stay after work? It's pretty odd."

"Yeah, I'll check it out. Is it some kind of weird medical tool?"

Julie raised her eyebrows, her smile strange.

"I don't know what it is yet... except for a very large, black machine."

3 - SUBJECT

After eight hours of processing almost one hundred customer orders and responding to emails, I finally clocked out to go to the warehouse to see the machine. As one of the company's lead mechanical and software technicians, Julie had already spent most of the afternoon working on it, but she'd told me through text she had made little progress.

I left the main building through a back door and crossed the employee parking lot before I reached the side door of the warehouse. It opened easily after twisting the knob, and the musty smell of the large space immediately filled my nose once I stepped inside. The yellow lights hanging from the ceiling hummed quietly, and most of the wide space was filled with tall, metal shelves holding labeled boxes and random medical equipment. I closed the door and followed the faint sound of music to a back corner of the warehouse, where I found Julie and the machine.

She stood in front of a laptop that sat on an unfolded plastic table, and the laptop had several wires trailing from it to the tall black machine ten or so feet away. Despite wanting to greet Julie and make my presence known, my gaze lingered on the machine, which filled me with a strange, unexpected eeriness.

"Jeremy!" Julie shouted, causing me to flinch. "You scared the daylights out of me."

I blinked, finally looking at her as she turned the music down on the laptop.

"Sorry," I said with a grin. "I wasn't trying to be sneaky—just surprised by that machine. I didn't think it would be creepy."

"It kind of is, isn't it?" Julie replied thoughtfully. "It was dropped off this weekend by a home restoration company. Apparently they got it from a house that burned down a week ago."

"Seriously? What about the owner?"

"I don't know—it's rare that we get equipment donated from residential properties, but it's usually because the owner died or abandoned everything."

"Okay. What does it do?"

"I'm not really sure. It has accelerators to generate radiation like a radiation therapy machine, but they're not built the standard way. Plus there's a metal platform inside it big enough for a human with leather straps, so... definitely creepy. This machine isn't anything a medical facility would ever use."

"Maybe it's the invention of a mad scientist, then."

"Yeah, that's the best theory right now," Julie said with a laugh. "I've been able to turn it on, but a lot of its components have smoke and heat damage, so I'm not sure how well it will work. It has a software program that I've been able to access, but it constantly glitches and none of the commands get a response from the machine."

I furrowed my eyebrows, looking back at the tall, daunting device. The outline of the door was difficult to see because of how well it blended into the body, and a chilling impulse made me want to touch the machine and see inside it.

"Ready to look inside?"

As if she knew what I felt, Julie had asked the perfect question. I blinked, staring at her as dread seeped into me.

"No—I'm good. That thing creeps me out and it should probably be turned into scrap metal."

Julie shoved my shoulder playfully and rolled her eyes.

"It will be scrap metal in a few weeks if I can't get it working and figure out what it's meant for. But I think it's fascinating as much as it is creepy. Are you sure you don't want me to open it?"

"Yeah. I'd rather get dinner—if you're hungry?"

Julie sighed, and I smiled innocently. Although I knew she had been on a dating break for a while, I always hoped she would end it, or at the very least, let me enjoy her company outside of work on occasion.

"Fine, we can grab dinner tonight. But I'm *not* dating right now."

"I know, Julie. No strings attached—I promise."

She smiled a little, tucking a strand of hair behind her ear. Despite looking like an angel to me, Julie was as mysterious as the black machine, in a way. Whatever reason she had for not dating she wouldn't say, and I found that out the first time I formally asked her on a date months ago. Of course, I considered that she just might not want to date *me* and faked some no-dating scenario for easy rejection—but even brushing the subject had brought tears to her eyes.

Whatever the reason was, it was real.

And maybe why she supported visions more than mind-reading.

● ● ● ● ● ●

A week later, I went to see Julie in the warehouse again after work. The day was gloomy and overcast as I stepped outside and eventually crossed into the building, where Julie had spent the last several days trying to fix the machine.

I hadn't seen her much while she worked on it, and from a few texts, I knew that progress had been slow.

When I made it to the back corner of the warehouse, I saw Julie kneeling along the right side of the machine with a flashlight in her hand, but after a minute, she stood and sighed.

"Everything seems to be hooked up properly, but other than getting the lights to turn on inside, I can't get anything else to work."

"Like what?"

"The computer program has a scanning function, but I can't get the machine to scan anything I put inside it. I've tried a coffee cup, a broom and even a branch with leaves, but nothing happens when I initiate."

"Could the machine want something human-sized, or shaped?" I asked curiously.

Julie shrugged and ran a hand through her hair.

"You think it's that complicated? Any machine with a scan function—even a medical one—should scan anything you put inside it."

"Yeah, but this machine is weird and probably cursed. Maybe we should try an old training dummy just in case? I'm sure there's one lying around here somewhere."

"Fine, but if that doesn't work, then the machine *will* be going to the junkyard next week. My boss won't let me work on it much longer, and I'll lose my bonus if it doesn't go to auction."

"Understood. Let's start looking."

We both turned and walked toward the metal shelves in the middle of the warehouse. Julie and I split up as we entered different aisles to begin searching, and I rummaged through several long, horizontal boxes hoping to find a dummy inside. But after twenty minutes, I only found a detached, plastic leg.

"Jeremy! I found one!"

Julie's excited shout caused me to race out of my aisle and into hers, where I saw her holding a nude training dummy with adjustable limbs. The dummy looked as though the top of its head and chest could be opened, and the color of its eyes and lips were faded, along with a few patches of hair that remained after what seemed like years of use and storage.

"It's not pretty, but it's perfect," I said with a grin.

Julie nodded quickly and I followed her back to the machine, my blood suddenly racing. When we stood in front of it, Julie pressed a button to the right of the door, causing it to pop open a few inches before she opened it entirely. For the first time, my gaze fell inside the bright, white interior and glided over six cylindrical collimators, as well as the stainless steel slab in the center. My eyes widened as I imagined someone strapped to the steel platform—likely against their will to endure whatever power the machine had. And that nightmare quickly felt real as I held the training dummy in place while Julie secured it with the leather straps.

"If this isn't a normal therapy machine, then it must be torture device," I said, half-joking.

"It could be," Julie replied ominously, stepping back from the dummy. "If you dose someone with enough radiation, they'll have terrible symptoms and die in just a few days."

A chill ran down my spine as I decided not to ask for more details, though my imagination filled in the gaps.

When we returned to the table with the laptop, I saw a program on the screen that had a large, black rectangle on the left side and a series of buttons and gauges on the right. At the top, one of the buttons read SCAN in red letters, and Julie looked at me after resting her hand over the mouse.

"I hope you're right," she said with a hint of desperation.

"Me too. Click it now."

Julie bit her lip as her gaze flashed to the screen, and within seconds, the soft *click* of the mouse filled the air. Nothing seemed to happen at first, until the top of the dummy's head started to appear inside the black rectangle, followed by the neck, shoulders, and more of its body while the scan ran.

"Yes!" Julie shouted, clapping her hands as she jumped happily. "It's finally scanning! Maybe the accelerators and collimators will work, too."

I grinned, basking in a surge of pride.

When SCAN COMPLETE appeared, Julie hovered over the ACCELERATOR 1 button and looked at me again.

"I just want to see if I can activate one of them," she said. "I don't really want to make the dummy radioactive."

"Yeah—let's avoid that. Can you activate an accelerator without creating a radiation beam?"

"I think so. The gauges above each button will show the strength of the beam through the collimators, so there has to be a way to control the intensity—meaning it could be at zero."

"Okay. Go for it."

Julie clicked the first accelerator button, and I hardly knew what to expect as we waited in silence. But to our mutual horror, NO SUBJECT DETECTED suddenly appeared across the screen, causing Julie to groan loudly.

"No! This is the same message I got earlier when I was trying to scan the other items. Why is it rejecting the dummy now? Maybe this stupid thing does belong in a junkyard. None of this makes any sense!"

I frowned while Julie buried her face in her hands, my pride now crushed by disappointment.

"Does the machine have a temperature reader?" I blurted. "Maybe that's the problem—it needs to sense a human in size and temperature before everything will work."

Julie sighed and shrugged.

"I haven't checked for that, but it's not safe to test with a real person right now."

"You sure? I'll go inside for a minute."

Julie's eyes widened as she stared at me, and I shrugged.

"It's probably a stupid thing to do, but how much damage could happen in a minute? If the gauges start moving, just shut the machine off."

Julie blinked, her expression mixed with emotion.

"Well, I *can* control whether it's running or not through the program, but..."

"So, let's do it. No need to lose your bonus over a real pound of flesh."

"Jeremy—you're crazy!"

"Get ready, okay?"

I left the table and quickly walked toward the machine, pressing the small button beside the door to open it. While I worked to free the dummy, I tried to ignore the eerie feeling I still had with rational thought: the machine wasn't really cursed, and if the program failed, Julie could simply unplug the wires.

I took a deep breath and tossed the dummy aside, then stepped in toward the bright lights.

4 - YELL

There wasn't much room to stand inside the machine, so I leaned back against the metal platform and slid my feet on top of the footrest. When I looked at Julie, her mouth formed a thin line, and despite my nerves, I tried to look calm and confident.

I saw her glance at the laptop and type before the machine door began to close. It moved slowly as it glided back into place, and my heart pounded as the world outside gradually disappeared. After a minute, I was totally trapped inside the machine, the bright lights still glowing all around me. I squinted and stared at the back of the machine door, focusing my attention on a red light inside a small circle of black glass.

The light began to flash and lasted for about thirty seconds—making me wonder if I was being scanned.

When it stopped, I looked at the three collimators on my left and right, noticing that each had a small circular opening blocked by a metal slat. My blood raced as I waited to see or hear a clue that the accelerators connected to them were activating, but minutes passed and nothing happened.

In an effort to stay calm and focused, I took a deep breath and closed my eyes.

How sick will I get if a radiation beam strikes me for a few seconds? What if Julie can't—

My thoughts froze as I finally heard a soft mechanical sound to my left. I jerked my head toward the three collimators on the curved wall, noticing the highest and closest one to my head had retracted its metal slat. Nothing but darkness was visible inside the narrow opening at first, and I stared at it tensely until a blue light appeared. The hair on the back of my neck stood on end as the blue light flashed a few times before it abruptly disappeared behind the metal slat.

I furrowed my brow as I tried to make sense of what just happened, though a terrifying possibility sent a chill down my spine.

Was I dosed with radiation?

But I hardly had a chance to think further before the door of the machine popped open, filling me with relief. I left the inner chamber as soon as I could and saw Julie smiling at me as she walked around the laptop and table.

"How did it go in there?" she asked curiously. "The accelerators activated, but it looks like nothing else happened."

"They all activated?" I asked, trying not to panic. "A collimator near my head flashed a blue light at me, but that's the only weird thing. Did you see any radiation being emitted?"

"No—none at all," Julie replied, shaking her head. "After you were scanned, the program said SUBJECT READY and the gauges above the accelerator buttons lit up, but I didn't see any beams triggered."

I ran a hand through my hair as I struggled with what to believe.

"Well, maybe there was a beam and the system failed to report it. I don't feel strange right now, but I guess that doesn't matter since radiation poisoning has delayed effects."

Julie made a skeptical noise and frowned.

"Don't say that—you're going to be just fine."

"I'm never going in there again."

"Of course not. But at least we know the machine seems to work."

I nodded slowly, haunted by the flashing blue light still.

"Are you sure no radiation generated?" I insisted.

"I mean—I guess I can't be certain, but I doubt anything happened to you."

Julie took my hand in hers, giving it a tight squeeze. I sighed, her touch helping my mood a little.

"Yeah, maybe not. I'm ready to go home."

"Me too. Cheer up, okay?"

· · · · · ·

My apartment building in the middle of town looked extra dull on a gloomy day. It certainly wasn't the nicest place to live, but with cheap rent and a fifteen minute commute to work, I wasn't going to be picky about it.

After unlocking the main door to the building, I stepped into the entryway, which had resident mailboxes lining the wall and stairs leading to the second and third floor. My gaze drifted across the faded orange walls and blue apartment doors while I traveled upward, headed toward my own place on the third floor. During the drive home, I'd managed to half-convince myself that nothing happened inside the machine, and that the accelerator had failed to do whatever it tried to execute.

It was a comforting thought, and it worked, sometimes.

When I reached the third floor, a hallway with four doors on either side stretched in front of me with a narrow, rectangular window at the end. My apartment was inside the third door on the right, but just as I got close to the second door on the left, a desperate male voice behind it stopped me.

I blinked, listening curiously.

"She found the syringe!" he shouted, his voice unmuffled. "What's going to happen when she sees the money is gone? I can't hide the problem—she's smart and she'll know why I took it. I never should have tried heroin when I was nineteen, because now I'm just a loser twelve years later who can't even make the rent! She'll never forgive me—she never will—and I'll end it all tonight if I have to."

My jaw dropped as I stared at the old, thin wooden door to the man's apartment, hardly able to believe how loudly he shared his confession for anyone to hear. My blood raced as I waited for another voice, but after a length of silence, I wondered if he was on the phone.

I need to get out of here—I hope he gets some help.

I quickly walked from the door and into my own apartment, where I locked the deadbolt and hung my jacket in the closet. I tried to forget what the man said as I went to the kitchen, but his problems haunted me more than my own while I made a quick dinner.

He needs some professional help, but I don't think he's going to do anything about that... and what's going to happen later tonight? Is he going to...

I shook my head and stared into a pot of canned soup on the stove. Death was frightfully easy to think about that day, and I didn't want to dwell on whether my neighbor—who I'd never met—would make it through the night, though I hoped whoever he spoke to had managed to calm him down.

After the soup started to boil, I poured it into a bowl and crushed a few crackers on top, then went to the couch to try to relax. I ate while I flipped through the TV channels, feeling a little better when I found a rerun of one of my favorite movies. But once I finished the soup and watched the movie for a while, my eyelids began to droop. At some point, I fell into a good sleep—until it ended abruptly with a gunshot.

I immediately sat on the edge of the couch, my heart pounding as I tried to come to my full senses.

Without a doubt, the shot had come from my disturbed neighbor's apartment, and as I reached for my cell phone on the coffee table, a second shot rang out.

What the hell is going on?

I grabbed my cell and dialed 911, telling the operator about the gunshots and their location. She told me a few policemen were already in the area and would arrive within minutes. When I ended the call, I took a deep breath and waited in horror for possibly another shot. But ten minutes passed without much sound, and I eventually heard the voices of a few police officers in the hallway. They banged on the door of the disturbed man's unit, and a moments later, a hysterical woman answered.

I stood and walked to my door, opening it slightly to peek down the hall. A short distance away, I saw a woman in a tank top and jeans talking to an officer, telling him through tears that her boyfriend had gotten upset about money and shot at their bedroom wall. While I watched, two other officers soon exited the apartment with a cuffed middle-aged man between them. I caught a glimpse of his bald head, black t-shirt and shorts before they disappeared, and he seemed to go quietly.

I closed my door and went back to the couch, sighing heavily as I checked the time. My cell phone screen read 11:39 PM, and I frowned, doubting I would get any decent sleep before work tomorrow. After shutting off the TV, I walked to the bathroom to get ready for bed, but a sudden knock on my door interrupted me.

I blinked as I looked in the mirror, waiting a few seconds before I crossed back into the living room. At the door, I looked through the peephole, surprised to see a police officer standing in front of it. I quickly opened the door and tried to look calm despite the earlier insanity.

"Hello," he said, his voice deep and firm. "Are you Jeremy Gregory?"

"Yeah—I made the 911 call."

"Precisely. We have the situation under control now, but is there anything else you heard or observed aside from the gunshots?"

I nodded slowly.

"When I came home from work, I heard that guy yelling inside the apartment. I think he was talking on the phone, but he said he took some money and that his girlfriend would find out what it was for. He also said something about heroin and 'ending it all' tonight."

"Okay, very good. Are you sure it was him yelling?"

I blinked, then furrowed my brow.

"It had to be. What he said lined up with what his girlfriend just reported."

"I understand, but that's interesting. When we spoke to him, his voice was hardly louder than a whisper because of his trach breathing tube."

"What? I mean, I never saw him, but that had to be his voice through the door," I replied, shocked. "I didn't hear anyone else talking."

"Okay, well, I'll make a note of that and look more into it, but that's all for tonight. Things should be a lot quieter around here."

The officer turned, walking away from my door as I closed it. Although I could hardly believe what he said about the trach tube... I knew I hadn't imagined what I'd heard.

5 - HEAR

Not long after I arrived at work the next morning, Julie made her usual visit to my cubicle. But instead of smiling at her, I stared dully at the computer screen, wishing I had taken the day off.

"What's wrong?" she asked immediately.

"Life," I replied flatly. "I can't believe the situations I've been in lately. Last night, my neighbor tried to shoot his girlfriend and the cops were called."

"Are you kidding? Why?"

"Because he took some money and bought drugs with it. I heard him shouting about it through the apartment door when I got home last night and I called 911 when I heard gunshots a few hours later. But here's the thing—when the police questioned me, he said I couldn't have heard the guy shouting because he has a trach tube. He can only speak in a loud whisper."

When I finally looked at Julie, she wore a frown and furrowed her eyebrows.

"Could you have heard someone else?"

"No, I didn't. The man was confessing to what he did, so it had to be him. Maybe he can shout but the police don't know that yet."

"He was arrested, right?"

"Yeah. And to top it all off, I still have Oliver's birthday party next week. With the robbery and shooting, I have no idea how I'm going to make it through *that* without losing my sanity."

Julie sighed and stepped toward me, her hand rubbing my shoulder.

"I think you need a vacation," she said softly.

"That's not a bad idea."

"How about I bring over some Chinese food Friday night? I know you haven't had Kong Wong in a while."

Delighted, I smiled a little as I looked at her.

"Perfect. That will definitely help."

● ● ● ● ● ●

After work, I decided to spend an hour or so at the bar. Though it was rare for me to drink alone, I wanted an easy way to relax my nerves for a minute.

I drove to a hole-in-the-wall tavern ten minutes away and parked behind the building. The bar looked mostly empty as I walked toward the back door, entering into a long hallway that led me into the main serving area. An older man and a middle-aged woman sat at the bar a few stools apart, and I walked to the far end to sit and keep my distance.

Behind the bar, an older woman with a lot of makeup and wrinkles approached me in a red shirt, blue jeans, and black apron. She smiled warmly at me, and I forced a polite smile on my face.

"What can I get you, honey?"

"Just a glass of bourbon neat, please."

She nodded and turned away as I rested my chin on my palm, enjoying the quietness of the bar at the start of the week. The older man at the other end smoked while sipping at his beer bottle, and the woman near him scrolled on her cellphone with a mixed drink in front of her. Both seemed content in their own worlds, and as I tried settling calmly into mine, the woman on her phone suddenly looked alarmed.

I furrowed my brow as I watched her read something for a minute, then quickly type a response back. The bartender approached me with the bourbon, and after she set it down, I heard the other woman speak.

"How was I supposed to know it was a treasured heirloom? I doubt the pawn shop has it anymore."

I looked up from my glass at her, but the woman continued staring at her phone, and neither the older man or bartender seemed to acknowledge that she spoke. I blinked and took a sip of the bourbon, distracted for a moment by the burn in my throat before a spicy maple aftertaste.

She just vented out loud... a lot of people do that here with all kinds of confessions and secrets...

"I guess I'll tell her Kinsey must have grabbed it and lost it—that's exactly what a four year old would do. She's always playing in the basement and she could have easily gotten into that box in the storage closet..."

My eyes widened in horror and fascination as I watched the woman begin to type on her phone. Although I heard her voice, I never once saw her lips move. But the voice had the right direction and distance to belong to her, and the confessions matched her sudden disturbance and gradual relaxation.

The woman smiled and set her phone on the bar top, grabbing her mixed drink to take a few sips. Thankfully, she didn't seem aware that my eyes were glued to her, and I waited to hear her voice again—as if it belonged to her thoughts.

"I'll say I saw Kinsey with the box and that she was playing with everything inside it before I found her and cleaned up the mess. There's a million places that necklace could be hiding down there if I hadn't taken it. I wish it wasn't something important to the family, but I didn't know."

I finally tore my eyes from the woman and tried to finish my bourbon. Although hearing thoughts was impossible, I couldn't find a way to easily deny what I had experienced. But while my anxieties grew, my heart pounded as I broke into a sweat, suddenly considering if I had somehow become mentally ill.

How does someone first realize they're schizophrenic? It's because they're hearing voices, right?

My gaze flashed to the old man across the bar with a beer and cigarette, but after thirty seconds, I couldn't hear a word of what might be on his mind. I furrowed my eyebrows as I looked back at the lying woman, but while she scrolled on her phone, I didn't hear her voice again, either.

Maybe it was just the alcohol. I don't know how, but that had to be it...

"Want another bourbon?"

The older woman behind the bar stood in front of me, and I shook my head, frowning.

"Can you think of a number between one and ten?"

"What? Why?"

"Please?"

"Well, alright. I'm thinking of one now."

I nodded once and stared into her eyes, waiting to hear the number as clearly as if she had spoken it out loud. But after a drawn-out awkward silence, I shrugged and gave up.

"What was that all about?" the woman asked, laughing. "Are you a mind reader?"

I blinked and laughed nervously.

"No—apparently not. Maybe I lost my mind last week or I shouldn't drink bourbon."

"You're hearing voices?"

"I'm not sure what I've been hearing, but I should go. What do I owe?"

The older woman gave me a curious look and stated the price of my tab, which I quickly paid before I left.

6 - MACRO

When Friday night came, Julie walked straight to the couch with Kong Wong Chinese food and her black work bag after I let her into my apartment. She spread the food out on the coffee table and after I sat down next to her, we started eating and watching TV.

My thoughts drifted as I wondered about telling her what happened at the bar earlier that week, along with a few other disturbing confessions I'd heard since. But I still didn't have a way to explain how any of it happened, and if Julie thought I was crazy, I might finally lose my sanity.

I sighed silently and decided to ignore the impossible subject.

"So... I think something happened to you inside the machine."

I blinked and stared at Julie, swallowing a bite of sweet and sour chicken.

"Are you serious? Why?"

"I've been able to dive a lot deeper into the operating software and I found a radiation emission log that the machine seems to automatically update. The last one recorded on the same day you went inside the machine, and it registered a low level emission that lasted about three seconds."

Julie's concerned expression became serious, and as the silence dragged on, I felt the urge to finally confess the impossible subject.

"I guess I'm not totally surprised," I admitted. "As much as I hate to hear that... it might explain something really weird that's been going on with me."

Julie raised her eyebrows as horror filled her face.

"What is it, Jeremy? Are you feeling alright?"

"Not exactly—but you're going to think I'm crazy when I tell you. I've wondered if I am a few times."

"You're not crazy and I don't care. Please, tell me."

"Okay, well—a few times this week, I've heard some people speak without their mouths moving, and I don't know how, but... I think I'm hearing their thoughts."

Julie's mouth fell open a little before she furrowed her brow.

"What? Are you sure?"

"Positive. The first time it happened, I went to the bar after work and heard this woman talk—*think*—about how she is going to blame a toddler for losing jewelry she stole. Her actions and expressions lined up with everything, and when she finally did speak out loud, the voice was the same."

"And you said it's happened again since?"

"Yes. You think I've lost my mind, don't you?"

"No—I believe you."

Her tone had a genuine ring of sincerity I didn't expect, but also struggled to accept.

"Why do you believe me so easily? Reading minds is impossible!"

Julie set her carton of fried rice on the coffee table and turned toward me with a knowing smile.

"Remember the radiation emission log? Well it also revealed the name of the radiation that the machine generates, which is Macro-molecule radiation. According to a college paper I found, it could be capable of all kinds of things because of its ability to change DNA."

"A college paper? That's it?"

"Yeah, I couldn't find anything else, but it was a PDF from an online archive of Strathsmith University. It was written by a man named Paul Henderson, and given the lack of information anywhere else online about Macro-molecule radiation, he must be involved with the creation of the machine."

Julie reached for the large black bag leaning against the coffee table and pulled out her laptop. Once she opened it, she set it on the coffee table, and a PDF essay filled the screen.

"This is the paper I found," she said excitedly, confirming my suspicion. "Paul theorized that Macro-molecule radiation could target DNA precisely enough to mutate it for changing physical appearance without damaging any bone marrow, organs, or having any other fatal effect. There's even a paragraph where he talks about how it could solely affect the brain. He said it could possibly make our sensory tissues and processes much more sensitive to the outside world for gathering information. So, given what you've been through this week... I think he was right. Your brain must be able to perceive and read the brainwaves of others at times."

"I guess so—but where is this guy now?"

"I'm not sure because I couldn't find much on him either. Besides being a student at Strathsmith, I found an article that mentioned him as an employee for a research lab that shut down, but that's it."

I nodded once, and we sat in silence for a minute, both of us seeming to try to make sense of all the pieces to this incredibly odd situation. But like a strike of lightning, I suddenly had my own revelation.

"Wait a second," I said, jumping up from the couch. "Julie, what if—what if I didn't hear my neighbor shouting? What if I heard his *thoughts*?"

Julie's eyes widened as she stared at me, the obvious truth now flooding through her.

"Jeremy—you did! You had too! The police said he couldn't speak above a whisper because of the trach tube."

"Exactly! So he was the first person I heard and not the woman at the bar—I just had no way of knowing it yet, but that explains everything."

Julie also stood and faced me, her brow furrowed in determination.

"Try reading my mind right now," she said firmly, closing her eyes.

I nodded and focused on her impatiently, but after more than twenty seconds, I heard nothing.

"Think about something bad," I suggested. "Those are the kinds of thoughts I've been able to hear so far. Maybe my brain tissue is only sensitive to that kind of energy."

Julie nodded and closed her eyes again, but after a full minute, I still heard nothing.

"What did you think about?" I asked, breaking the silence.

"I was thinking about robbing a store, and then I thought about stealing a car," she replied. "You didn't hear a word of it?"

"No."

"So you can only hear bad thoughts, but not all the time. I wonder what triggers it?"

I shrugged and lowered myself back down on the couch, which Julie did as well.

"I wish we knew more about that Paul guy. I have tons of questions for him," I said at length.

"Me too. I wonder if it was his house that burned down with the machine in it."

We reached for our food and started eating again. A movie played on the TV that I had seen a few times before, and just as I was about to ask Julie if she'd seen it, she spoke.

"He looks a lot like Dan. I hope he's doing well."

I looked away from the TV and at her.

"Dan?"

Julie blinked, then stared at me.

"What?"

"Whose Dan? You said that actor looks like him."

Julie blinked again, her expression riddled with disbelief.

"He's just someone I used to know well," she replied quickly. "I—I shouldn't have mentioned it."

"It's okay. Did something happen to him?"

"He's alright," Julie said, rising from the couch. "I think I should go—I'm full and tonight has been a bit overwhelming."

I frowned, my brow furrowed in confusion as I watched her quickly grab her things and head for the door. Normally I would have walked her out, but it seemed to be the last thing she wanted at that moment. Julie turned before she left and said goodbye, then vanished. I wasn't sure why her demeanor had suddenly changed, but after a few minutes to myself, I doubted she had mentioned Dan aloud at all.

7 - SECRET

Saturday morning, I walked lazily to the kitchen after climbing out of bed. I put on a pot of coffee and rubbed my eyes, trying to clear my brain fog as I thought about last night. But after a few minutes, I wasn't sure why I could hear the bad thoughts of the woman at the bar and not Julie's.

Maybe I couldn't hear her because her thoughts weren't genuine? Ugh, doubt it...

I soon poured a cup of coffee and carried it to the couch, settling in for a deeper round of thinking. The truth to my hearing trigger seemed within reach, and if I carefully examined everything I had heard so far, I felt like I could crack the code—or come close.

My neighbor freaked out about drugs and the money he took, and the bar woman wanted to frame a kid for the necklace she stole... so maybe I can hear confessions, or... secrets?

I furrowed my brow as I sipped at my coffee, remembering the research paper written by the mysterious Paul and what it said about brain tissue sensitivity. Although it seemed like a stretch to believe a machine could somehow make me able to hear people's secrets, the fact that I could hear them at all made me want to believe it.

If each emotion has a different energy, then maybe I'm sensitive to the energy tied to most secrets or whatnot. I need to hear a lot more thoughts before I can be sure.

I rose from the couch when I finished my coffee and rinsed the cup in the kitchen. Despite feeling a little terrified, I decided to walk the street for a long day of thought hunting.

· · · · · ·

The bright sun helped my mood when I stepped out of my apartment building later that morning. I turned left and walked toward the north side of town, hoping I wouldn't go more than a few blocks before I heard the voice of a new mind.

The streets were decently crowded while I walked with my gaze pointed at the pavement. I felt rude and awkward for seeking out more private thoughts, but like the woman at the bar, I might not even know the name of the next stranger, which helped a little.

I walked for ten minutes before I finally heard the voice of a man on a bench several yards in front of me. He stared at a newspaper and seemed to be reading it, but his mind raced on while his lips remained motionless.

Maybe it wasn't right, but he died a quick death at his favorite spot by the pond. I had to pull the trigger... I don't think Charlie would have asked for anything different. He died at home without any more suffering...

I blinked after a minute of staring at the man from a short distance away—my heart pounding as I tried to understand what had happened to Charlie. But I soon became aware of myself and shifted into an alleyway, where I waited out of sight for any more revealing thoughts.

We had the best nine years together... he didn't deserve to die in a vet's office. Some people might think I'm terrible if I told them what I did, but his life ended at home, where he was born...

I sighed heavily in relief once I realized the man must be thinking about a pet—most likely a dog. I frowned and walked through the alley to the other side of the block, where I felt even more dread and fascination about the next confession I might hear. But it wasn't too long before I came upon a restaurant with outdoor seating, and I saw two women sitting at a table, one of them listening while the other cried.

"I don't know what happened—I thought everything was going so well," the woman in a purple shirt said, wiping her eyes with a napkin. "Do you know why they fired me? The manager wouldn't say anything other than 'it wasn't working out.' I can hardly believe that."

"I have no idea what happened," the second woman replied in a pink sundress. "Jobs can be cruel like that sometimes, but you'll get another one—a much better one. I promise."

She reached out and took the other woman's hand, her face full of sympathy. And I would have believed her, until I suddenly heard her voice again, though she wasn't speaking aloud.

I really need a raise and they couldn't afford it without letting someone go... I'm sorry but I had to give you a terrible review.

"You're right, I *will* get a better job and I won't be treated like this again," the purple shirt woman replied. "If you don't mind being one of my references, I would greatly appreciate it."

"Of course, no problem. Cheer up, okay?"

My sadness toward the beloved pet vanished as anger flooded me, and I quickly crossed the street, fighting the urge to shout the truth at the betrayed woman. But despite the power I had to discover lies and secrets... I wasn't sure I had the right to intrude on the lives of perfect strangers.

By the time I returned home later that day, I no longer had a doubt about the trigger I needed to hear a mind speak.

• • • • • •

I eagerly dialed Julie's number when she was free for a call that evening. My blood raced while the line rang, but she finally answered on the fourth ring.

"Jeremy?" she said. "What's up?"

"Hey—so I spent the afternoon walking around the city to hear more thoughts, and I think I figured out the trigger."

"Really? What is it?"

"I think I hear secrets—dark secrets. That explains everything I've heard so far, and why I couldn't hear your thoughts the other night when we tried to test it."

Julie gasped slightly, and I imagined her expression full of surprise.

"I guess that makes sense. What did you hear while you were walking around?"

"Well, I heard some guy convincing himself it was okay to shoot his old dog, and then I heard a woman thinking about how she got her friend fired for a raise. I heard more than that before I came home, and it was pretty depressing."

"Yeah... I can imagine."

"I figured out something else, too. I have to be within twenty feet or so of someone to hear their mind, or else their thoughts fade like a normal voice."

"That's interesting. How often are people thinking about their darkest secrets? At least you won't be bombarded with thoughts all the time."

"True. I hate to ask, but—who was Dan?"

Her end of the line fell silent while I waited, though I started to wonder if I should have brought it up.

"He used to be very special to me—I don't want to talk about it, okay?"

"Oh sure, no problem. I was just curious."

"That's okay. I'll see you Monday?"

"Yeah, see you then."

When our call ended, I stared at the phone, intrigued by what could be Julie's secret.

8 - SHAME

After all I had been through lately, the morning of Oliver's birthday still felt tough. My memories of us always felt the most vivid on his birthday, and my thoughts of what it would be like to have an adult brother around my age felt particularly painful.

I parked behind the vehicles of my aunt, uncle and sister at my parents house and made my way to the front door. Inside the foyer, I heard voices and sounds coming from the dining room and kitchen area, so I slid off my jacket and walked into the kitchen.

My dad and uncle leaned against the counter near each other as they talked and sipped from short glasses of whiskey. Both were tall men with graying brown hair and each wore a sweater with jeans. My sister, Sara, talked on her cell phone in front of the stove, and she stood shorter than me with dyed blonde hair. She waved and I smiled at the three of them before looking left into the dining room, where I saw my mother and aunt setting the dinner table.

A small white box sat on top of the counter near my uncle, and I knew what would be inside before I looked through the clear plastic top. A round cake with white frosting sat inside and had "Happy Birthday Oliver" written in green cursive letters on top of it. Since the first anniversary of his disappearance, we always bought a similar looking cake, and the one last year had white frosting and red cursive letters.

"I never should have let him out of my sight around that strange couple," my father said, catching my attention suddenly. "What if losing that precious boy is my fault?"

"Of course it's not, Neil," my uncle replied, as he had many times through the years. "How could you and Diane possibly know what would happen? It's possible that couple had nothing to do with his absence, and I highly doubt there was anything you could do about it. Kids run around campgrounds all the time—it's perfectly normal."

My father nodded slowly, but the hurt in his eyes told me he hardly felt convinced. My chest began to ache as I tried to think of something to brighten his mood.

"Remember when you took us to the men's breakfast our first morning there?" I said excitedly. "The bacon, eggs, and biscuits were so good, and then we learned a lot of basic survival skills from the camp ranger. We loved every minute of that."

My dad smiled a little, the look in his eye relaxing as he silently seemed to relive the memory with a thoughtful expression. The ache in my chest faded now that my mission had succeeded, and my uncle started talking about another fun memory of my dad and Oliver at the middle school baseball field. I grinned while I listened, soon noticing my sister finally pull her cell phone away from her ear.

"Hey, Jeremy," Sara said with a smile. "I didn't mean to be stuck on the phone, but that was my friend Abby. Remember the crazy patient I told you escaped the hospital several weeks ago?"

"Oh, um—that Dana girl?"

"Yeah. I mean, no one knows who she really is, but yes—*her*. Our boss is livid because the police are still refusing to look for her even though she needs some serious mental health treatment. The police are saying she had no legal obligation to stay there, so she could leave any time she wanted."

"Well, if she's an adult, then yeah—she can't be held captive there, even if she needs help."

"I know, but it's sad. I wonder why she tried to claim the identity of a missing person? Either she's mentally ill or there is something fishy the police *should* be looking into. Guess they don't care enough."

I frowned and shrugged, and Sara slid her phone into the pants pocket of her purple scrubs, her expression disturbed.

"Is everyone ready?" my aunt said in a raised voice from the dining room.

My uncle grabbed the cake box and the three of us left the kitchen. After passing into the dining room, my sister and I stood on one side of the table, while my dad and uncle stood across from us. My uncle took the cake from the white box and set it on a silver platter in the middle of the table, then my mother started to stick thin candles into it. I counted them until she placed nineteen individual candles into the frosting—the age Oliver would be now if he were still alive.

I sighed quietly while my mother silently lit the candles, and afterward, we all sang happy birthday before each of us blew out some of the small flames. We all settled into our seats as my dad walked back to the kitchen and returned with a large pan of lasagna. Any hope I had of telling my parents what happened to me certainly seemed beyond reach that day, though I didn't mind letting the subject rest until the perfect moment—*somehow*—came.

While my family talked, I sat mostly quiet during the meal, listening and enjoying the mental silence. But toward the end as we neared dessert, my mother cleared her throat and suddenly spoke up.

"I wish I could tell you all what happened to Oliver... I've wanted too for so long."

Her shocking statement sent a chill down my spine, though her tone was soft and quiet. I looked up from my plate and stared at her, my horror intensifying as I watched her stare at the white table cloth thoughtfully, realizing she hadn't spoken aloud.

"Jeremy! Do you want a slice?"

I blinked and turned my head robotically toward Sara, who stood across from me and held a knife in the middle of the cake. But my response didn't seem to matter as she cut a thin slice and set it on the edge of my plate anyway.

I miss you so much, Oliver... your death would have been much worse the other way. I know what I did wasn't right, but maybe better...

The hair on the back of my neck rose as I could hardly believe the haunting confession that filled my mind and no one else's. Although I wanted to look at my mother again, I stared at the piece of cake my sister had given in a bad attempt to hide all the emotions that flashed across my face.

My mother knows what happened to Oliver!

Without thinking, I suddenly stood from the table, almost knocking over my water glass as I pushed my plate forward. My aunt flinched beside me in surprise, and my mother snapped out of her distant expression to look at me and furrow her eyebrows.

"Jeremy, are you okay?" she asked.

I tore my gaze away from her and took a step back, causing my chair to screech along the wood floor.

"I, um—I just need some air."

I ignored the surprise of the rest of my family and left the dining room through the kitchen, then headed for the foyer. There, I quickly jogged up the staircase to the guest bedroom on the second floor. It had a small balcony that faced a treeline thick enough to block out the neighboring house, and when I made it outside, I gripped the railing as I tried to catch my breath.

What has she hid all these years? My mother—she couldn't have had something to do with Oliver disappearing, I don't believe it, I—

Countless memories from ten long years of mourning passed through my mind, especially those of my mother being utterly wrecked in the beginning, and all the time and energy my dad, sister, and I had used to make sure she would be alright. But it all slowly started to make sense in a new and terrifying way.

All the tears, guilt, and sadness had been real.

Just not for the reasons any of us assumed.

Although I wanted to go back and try to learn more, I was still mortified by the truth, and I couldn't imagine her motive for taking part in ending the life of her own son.

Until I remembered the headaches.

9 - DOCK

I turned when the sliding glass door opened suddenly behind me, eyeing my sister as she stepped onto the porch.

"What's going on?" Sara asked, concerned. "Are you alright? We're worried about you."

"I've had one hell of a month," I blurted. "There's no way you'll believe what I've been through."

"What is it? Anything about Oliver?"

"No. Aside from the freak robbery, a weird machine was dropped off at work recently and I volunteered to go inside it for some simple testing, but... I haven't really been the same since."

"How?"

"Will you believe me if I tell you? I'm not kidding."

"Okay—what is it?"

"I can hear people when they confess bad things in their heads—like their dark secrets. I know it sounds crazy, but I can sometimes hear people think, and I left the dining room because..."

I squeezed my eyes shut as tears threatened to break loose. Even at family gatherings for Oliver, I didn't like to cry, but the horrifying truth of my mother's involvement went beyond what I could bear. After wiping my cheeks with my sleeve, I looked at Sara, who watched me with a shocked expression.

"Do you want to know what happened to Oliver?" I finally managed. "Our mother... she knows! I heard her thoughts, and I swear I'm not making it up—I swear."

Sara blinked and tucked a strand of hair behind her ear, her gaze falling away from mine.

"I don't know what you're going through, but mom isn't involved in what happened to Oliver—it's impossible, Jeremy."

"Just ask mom to meet me in the guest bedroom after our aunt and uncle leave, okay?"

"Why? Are you going to accuse her?"

"No! I just need to ask her some questions and see what she thinks, okay?"

My sister furrowed her eyebrows and sighed, then left the porch without answering me. I turned and gripped the railing hard, causing my knuckles to turn white. Whether she believed me I couldn't tell, but I was more concerned about how I would confront my mother without blind anger.

I won't start out blaming her... but what if she admits in her mind exactly what happened? How do I control myself then?

A crushing wave of shock and betrayal made me leave the balcony and find my way to the guest bed, which I curled on top of with a pillow pressed to my chest. As I lay there, I didn't mind if it took my mother a while to come into the room, because I needed to manage all the stress I felt first, though it seemed unlikely. More tears escaped as I lay motionless, hardly paying attention to the time that passed as I struggled through my own thoughts.

But it was sometime later that I heard the bedroom door creak open, and soon I felt a spot on the mattress sink down beside me.

"Jeremy," my mother said softly. "What's wrong? I worried for you earlier."

I sighed and turned to my back, feeling slightly better than I did a while ago. Although I wanted to sit up and feel less like a child, it seemed easier to keep my cool if I stared at the ceiling.

"This anniversary has been pretty rough," I told her, trying to keep my tone even. "After all these years... I still wish we knew something about what happened to Oliver—even if it was something small."

"Yes," she said, nodding her head. "I know."

I bit my lip and took a few deep breaths.

"Is there anything you know, mom?"

"Of course not. Though I hope the truth will come to us one day. Are you going to be alright?"

My gaze flashed to her, hardly knowing how to answer her question truthfully. I stayed silent as I waited to hear another thought-driven confession, but when none came, I felt undeterred.

"Mom... you know what happened to Oliver, don't you?"

I looked away from the ceiling and finally focused on her face, which showed a number of emotions.

"What?" she said, confused. "I already told you I don't know anything. If I did, you and everyone else would know it, too."

"That's not true at all."

My mother blinked and rose from the bed, staring down at me in shock.

"It's not important how I know, but the way Oliver died... you believe is best."

My mother gasped and clapped a hand over her mouth, horrified. I finally sat up and swung my legs over the side of the bed, my eyes stung by tears again.

"Please, mom—just tell me what happened. Did it have something to do with his headaches? I need to know what happened to him."

She shook her head and stepped backward, lowering her hand.

"Jeremy, I can't believe you're saying this to me!"

"I know you know the truth, mom, and you need to tell all of us!"

The fury I imagined would come felt impossible as I sank into a spiral of desperation, waiting for her to finally crack. My mother looked away as tears fell down her cheeks, and I noticed the sound of footsteps headed down the hall toward the bedroom door.

"What's going on?"

My dad's voice echoed into the room before he stepped inside with Sara behind him. I glanced at them before staring at my mother again, still determined to force the truth out of her.

"She knows what happened to Oliver," I stated. "She's known the truth all this time."

My mother remained silent as she looked at the floor, standing motionless. My gaze swept to my father and Sara, both of whom seemed a bit overcome with shock and surprise.

"Jeremy, slow down," my father said at length, his tone slightly shaken. "I don't know where you got the idea, but—"

"Oliver was never going to leave this world without pain."

My blood raced after my mother's sudden interruption. I watched as she wiped her cheeks and then looked at each of us with a calm expression; all her sadness from earlier seemingly controlled now rather than disappeared.

"Two days before our camping trip, I found out his bad headaches were caused by a brain tumor that the doctor said was too deep to operate on. So... I made the decision not to tell anyone. I wanted all of you to have the chance to make great memories before we had to come home and deal with what time he had left."

I could hardly think or feel as she spoke, but afterward, I felt a sense of relief toward my long-held suspicion of his abnormal headaches.

"Diane... how could you do this?"

My dad's voice sounded quiet and weak as he struggled to digest her confession. Sara stood behind him with her hand over her mouth, her eyes wide with shock and tears.

"It may not have been the best choice," she replied at length. "But there were no easy choices, Neil. It was the only way we could keep living happily and normally for a little while."

"Except that something happened to him at the campground and he died anyway," I replied angrily, standing from the bed. "How did he die, mom? Did you see someone take him, or did he fall, or—"

"He drowned."

Sara suddenly gasped as a chill shot down my spine. I vaguely noticed my father walk near me to sit down on the bed, as though standing had become too difficult.

"I wasn't at the bathhouse the afternoon Oliver went missing," my mother continued. "I was with him and we were at a large pond about half a mile into the woods from our campsite. We discovered it while on a nature walk, and Oliver wanted to play on the dock with his sharks and dinosaurs, so I let him."

My mother paused, using the sleeve of her sweater to wipe away more tears.

"I sat on the beach and went through pictures on our camera while he played on the dock, and next thing I know, he'd fallen into the water. I don't know how it happened, but the pond was deep, and he was struggling to swim. Of course I jumped up to help him, but then I thought about the tumor, and how it was going to cause him a lot of pain before it took him from us... and I froze—I couldn't bring myself to do anything for him. But my heart shattered forever that day and I don't expect any of you to understand it."

When she finished, my father, Sara and I tried to process all our thoughts and feelings in stunned silence. But it seemed impossible to try to make sense of the mother I *loved*—the one who cared for me almost perfectly my whole life—was capable of passively watching her son die.

"You watched him drown?" Sara asked, horrified.

My mother shook her head.

"He wasn't above the water very long. I believe he passed very quickly."

My father then rose from the bed, and I winced as I looked at him, seeing his face and eyes red.

"We'll talk about this later, Diane."

A throbbing pain started in my chest after he left the room, and Sara soon followed, leaving me alone with our mother without a word.

"I understand if none of you can ever forgive me," my mother said quietly. "But Oliver would have lived out the rest of his life in a hospital room, knowing that we were all sad and there was nothing we could do to save him. He should never have had that kind of pressure on his shoulders at such a young age. I don't like what happened, but it was an accident and spared a lot of pain. Either way... he deserved so much better."

I took a deep breath and closed my eyes, not wanting to believe there could be any justifications.

"How did you know, Jeremy?" she asked at length. "I've never told anyone or written it down anywhere."

I looked at her and frowned. The last thing I wanted to do now was to remember other people's horrors, and try to explain how a strange machine had given me the terrible ability to hear them. But like my mother's choice, hiding the truth had its advantages, and I wasn't ready to expose mine to her, yet.

"I'm sorry... but that's a secret worth keeping."

DARK UNION

ALLISON

1 - SESSION

The warm temperature in Reno brought a little comfort that morning as I walked from my car toward the front doors of the Mulden-Hale center. The mental health facility had two metal doors at the top of a short flight of cement steps, and the building itself stretched out wide on either side of the main entrance.

Although my first few weeks of counseling patients had gone well, the Mulden-Hale facility lacked all notions of warmth beyond its front doors.

After passing inside, I walked toward a glass window positioned between several gray locked doors. The receptionist sat behind the window at the front desk, and she was an older woman who I wasn't sure cared very much for me.

"Good morning," I said, trying to sound cheery. "Could you punch me in please? I'm—"

"Allison Collins," she said abruptly, her eyes on her computer screen. "I can remember who you are."

I nodded a little and shrugged.

"Okay. I won't say it again, then."

"Very good. The door to the offices is unlocked now."

"Sure—thank you."

I turned left and opened the first gray door, which felt heavy and had a small square window at the top. The long hallway on the other side had blue walls and several doors that led into private offices, and I walked to the third one on the right. After unlocking it, I stepped into my office and approached my desk and the narrow vertical window nearby. A couch with a large picture of a field above it sat across from my desk, and I found it comfortable for catching a quick nap in the afternoons.

Once I sat down behind my desk, I grabbed the first patient file lying across my keyboard and opened it, reviewing the notes I'd written from our session yesterday. Even though I thought Mulden-Hale was a dreary place even on a sunny day, I truly felt like I could make a difference as the days passed. By the time I moved on to the second file, I looked up after I heard a knock on my office door.

"Hi—come in!"

When it opened, I saw Dr. Michael Harris standing in the gap, his graying brown hair combed and wearing a black suit.

"Good morning," he said with a friendly grin. "How's it going, Allison?"

"Fine—just reading over some session notes to get ready for the day. How are you?"

"I'm well, thank you. If you have some time this afternoon, I was wondering if you wanted to sit in on one of my sessions. I think it would be useful to start getting you experienced with some of our more challenging patients."

"I can make time. Which one?"

"His name is Jeremy Gregory. He's one of our live-ins and he's been here a while. We don't have an official diagnosis for him yet, but he appears to have a history of delusion and schizophrenic episodes."

"Okay, I'd love to observe. What time?"

"His session is at two in room four."

"Perfect—I'll be there."

Dr. Harris nodded once and left the office, closing the door gently behind him.

• • • • • •

Fifteen minutes before two o'clock, I entered the front lobby and passed through the gray door that led to the therapy rooms and live-in patient quarters.

The therapy hall had six doors on the left and a line of bright windows on the right, and at the very end stood another gray door that required a special key code to unlock. The live-in patients were kept and attended to in their own rooms beyond it, and easily guided to their therapy appointments by a security officer. Although I was curious about their quarters, the thought of stepping inside their private rooms felt too close for comfort.

Room four looked like any of the other therapy rooms with a couch on one side and two stiff chairs on the other, along with a rectangular metal table in the middle. It had one large window in the center wall, and a picture of abstract pastel flowers above the couch. I settled into the chair closest to the window and laid my notebook on my lap, knowing Jeremy or Dr. Harris would arrive at any moment—though I hoped Jeremy would not be first. Despite taking the job at Mulden-Hale for the opportunity to work with behavioral patients, I had no experience from my last four years of counseling, and until I knew what I was doing... being alone with one of them seemed daunting.

For the next several minutes, I tried to calm my anxious anticipation in the noticeable silence of the room. But it finally eased when Dr. Harris suddenly entered and smiled at me.

"Early, of course," he said, a remark on my presence. "Jeremy, however, will not be. He hates our sessions and is usually ten minutes late."

"Oh—that's unfortunate. What's wrong?"

"He doesn't want to work past his perceived reality and into more healthy, positive thinking. He's utterly convinced of everything he told me when he first arrived and won't budge on it."

Dr. Harris closed the door and lowered into the chair beside me, holding his own notebook and patient file. I studied his face briefly, which looked tired.

"What happens if a behavioral patient can't be helped?" I asked, concerned.

"Honestly, there are few cases where I've felt like significant improvement was made without medication, but as long as they're here, we must always try to help them psychologically. Treating the root of a problem is better than only the symptoms."

"Yes, of course. What do you think Jeremy's root is?"

"Well—murder."

My eyes widened in shock while Dr. Harris laughed.

"Relax, Allison. His perception about what you will hear today isn't real. Jeremy is stuck inside a traumatic event that mental illness has twisted into a much darker reality for him."

I nodded slowly and swept my gaze to the couch, staring blankly as my anxiety spiked all over again. Dr. Harris occupied himself with Jeremy's file until the door opened a minute later and a security officer stepped in, followed by a younger man in a white t-shirt and gray sweatpants. He looked to be in his late twenties to early thirties, and he took a seat on the left end of the couch without any verbal instruction.

Jeremy stared at the floor with a bored expression while the security officer informed us he would remain outside the door and left. I glanced at Jeremy after, thinking he seemed too skinny to be healthy.

"Hi Jeremy," Dr. Harris said pleasantly. "How has today been for you?"

"Good," he said shortly.

"Really? What's been good about it?"

"Nothing, actually. My head still hurts all the time."

"I understand—we'll have a better idea about that after your MRI appointment soon. No new voices?"

"No... I don't think they're ever coming back."

I furrowed my eyebrows as I watched Jeremy, who gave no indication that he even noticed me in the room. But other than being underweight, he looked like a normal person I might encounter on the street, and so far, he didn't seem out of touch at all.

"Have you practiced any of the five methods of positively controlled thinking we discussed last week?"

Jeremy made a strange noise that sounded like a muffled laugh, and his right leg started to bob.

"You think I can forget that my mother is a confessed murderer with a little positive thinking? You must be crazy."

"Those methods are not for forgetting," Dr. Harris replied calmly. "But they will help you heal from your anger and trauma. There is no evidence of what you say your mother confessed to, so it is in your best interest to push past whatever lies the voices you used to hear told you. She did not kill your brother, Jeremy."

I almost gasped, but shifted uncomfortably instead while I clenched my teeth. Jeremy's expression darkened as he stared at Dr. Harris, and I could sense his anger blooming.

"She watched him drown! She and my father need to go to hell or prison—I don't care which one!"

Pain shot through my fingers as I tightly gripped the arm rest of my chair. Jeremy suddenly stood up, the look in his eyes blazing.

"Sit down now," Dr. Harris said, his tone a firm demand. "You are letting an unproven belief control you no matter how real it seems. I do *not* want to have another session with you in restraints. We have come a long way from that."

"But I'm not crazy! I heard her thoughts and she confessed it to me. I would have gotten it recorded, too, but I'm forced to be here. Oliver will never get justice if I'm locked away!"

My heart pounded as I expected Dr. Harris to order him to sit down again, but hardly a second passed before the security officer entered and approached Jeremy, who reluctantly submitted to handcuffs and being escorted from the room.

• • • • • •

As soon as the red clock in my office hit six o'clock, I gathered my things and left. Jeremy's outburst and removal still lingered on my mind as I exited the building and walked toward my car, but a large, black police SUV parked beside it distracted me.

Through the windshield, I saw officer Liam Garrett sitting in the driver's seat, his attention focused on the laptop toward his right. He had thick brown hair and scruff along his jaw, and I liked that his eyes looked almost golden in bright light. We had spoken a few times in passing when he escorted a court-ordered patient to the facility, and each time, I never saw a ring on his finger. I smiled a little and looked elsewhere—pretending not to notice him.

But just when I reached my car door, I heard his window roll down, then his voice.

"Hey, Allison."

I looked up, faking surprise.

"Oh—hi, Liam. Another drop off today?"

"Yeah, a late one. How's life?"

"Good, though a bit shocking this afternoon. I had a patient lose his temper and be removed from therapy in handcuffs."

Liam furrowed his brow and frowned.

"Are you alright?"

"Yeah."

"Did he come after you?"

"No, thankfully. I was just sitting in on his session, and Dr. Harris was with me."

"Good—glad to hear it. Headed home?"

"Yes, you?"

"Yeah, but I'll be back around here soon enough. Make sure I catch you to say hello, okay?"

I nodded while my cheeks grew warm.

"Of course. Have a good night, Liam."

"Thanks. Have a better one."

We smiled at each other before I climbed in my car, and he followed me out of the parking lot until we turned in different directions.

2 - FAVOR

Around seven o'clock that evening, I pulled into the driveway of my small ranch. It sat in the middle of a large neighborhood with many winding streets, and looked very similar to the other homes built in the sixties that surrounded it.

While I watched my garage door slowly rise, the counseling session with Jeremy still lingered on my mind. Although I believed schizophrenic episodes had worsened his past trauma like Dr. Harris concluded, I felt surprised by a persistent desire to believe him. But, I easily chalked it up to a lack of experience.

I feel bad so of course I want to believe him... but after enough time and more patients, I won't be so sensitive to their distress.

After parking inside the garage, I entered my house through a side door that led into a small mudroom. I hung my coat and purse on a peg in the wall across from the washer and dryer, then passed into the kitchen. I continued through to the living room and made my way to the master bedroom on the other side of the house. My door stood open from that morning, and I walked through scattered clothes on the floor to reach my closet on the left side of the bed. My bed sat against the wall in the center of the room with a nightstand on either side—one of which had a lamp and glass of water, and the other a stack of three books.

I grabbed a t-shirt and sweatpants from my closet, tossing them on my bed as I started to undress from my work clothes. Thankfully, I no longer feared seeing the dark scars that marred most of my legs, as my own years of therapy had helped me overcome my childhood trauma. But with Jeremy still on my mind, I stopped undressing when only my button-up blouse and underwear were left, and crossed the hall to the guest bedroom. In the corner near the door, a full-length oval mirror rested in a wooden stand, and I bravely stepped in front of it.

My gaze slowly drifted from my blonde hair and brown eyes to my bare legs, which had several long and short scars across the otherwise smooth, pale skin. Each scar had a dark purple color, though some of the smaller ones had faded more noticeably. Despite my psychological recovery from the horror I endured, I still kept my legs covered as much as possible, for the shocked look of strangers or sharing my story endlessly had grown tiresome.

My life had managed to return to normal since the day the scars were made, and all I wanted was to keep it that way.

• • • • • •

I met Dr. Harris for lunch after my first three counseling sessions the next day. The warm sun felt good against my skin while we sat at a table in the courtyard outside of the staff cafeteria. After a bit of small talk and discussing our schedule for the day, the conversation inevitably shifted to our session with Jeremy.

"What do you make of him?" Dr. Harris asked curiously. "I'd like to hear your thoughts now that you've had a little time to reflect on it."

I smiled a little and took a bite of my yogurt.

"I agree with your analysis of him, but I'm disturbed by the accusations he made against his mother. I realize they must be false, but was there ever an investigation?"

Dr. Harris sighed and shook his head.

"Jeremy was brought to us by the police shortly after he broke into his parents house and threatened them a few years ago," he replied. "He had a tape recorder and demanded that his mother confess to his brother's death or else he would do something bad to her and his father. Naturally, the police were called and Jeremy was deemed mentally unstable after a few days in jail. I've spoken to his mother about the incident, and she says he became obsessed with the idea that she had murdered his brother Oliver during the last birthday party they had to commemorate him. I believe he had a mental breakdown that day and hallucinated her original confession, though he also claims his father heard it and decided to act like it never happened."

"He does sound delusional," I said. "Why did he break-in?"

"Jeremy harassed his parents for a while after the birthday party until eventually they stopped letting him inside the house."

"Does he have other siblings?"

"Yes—a sister, but she moved to another state shortly before he was arrested. She has never answered my contact attempts."

I furrowed my eyebrows and looked down at my sandwich before taking a bite. Despite Jeremy being mentally ill, the layers of his complicated reality were fascinating.

"Why would he suddenly snap after ten years?" I asked. "It seems that would happen a lot sooner if he was deeply traumatized and unstable."

"I think the trigger for him was ultimately an attempted robbery he got caught up in before the birthday party. That incident has been verified and he wrestled the gunman to the ground himself. Obviously I cannot say for sure what snapped him, but two high stress events happening back to back could cause a breakdown."

Dr. Harris started to finish his salad while I let silence linger between us to gather my thoughts. I could see how Jeremy's diagnosis almost seemed impossible, for there were so many pieces to his past to consider.

"Are all behavioral patients this complex?" I asked with a small smile.

Dr. Harris laughed, wiping his mouth with a napkin.

"You will always find complexity with each of them, but Jeremy's case is very unusual."

"Of course! So, how does schizophrenia tie into all this? Do you think it was triggered by or a side effect of his breakdown at the birthday party?"

"It's hard to say, really. Jeremy says he began hearing voices before the party, and it happened because he went inside a strange machine at the medical supply company he used to work at. He claims the machine altered his brain and made him able to hear other people's thoughts."

"Is that true?"

Dr. Harris, who had pleasantly enjoyed our lunch and conversation, looked at me suddenly with concern. I smiled quickly as my cheeks burned, waving a hand dismissively.

"Of course not," I said. "But the machine—does it exist?"

"Perhaps it did, but he said it was sold two months after they received it. I suppose you could contact the company in order to track it down."

"Really? Do I just give them a call?"

Dr. Harris raised an eyebrow, and I realized I had fallen for his trick.

"You're starting to believe his stories, aren't you, Allison?"

The intense heat in my cheeks remained as I shrugged.

"No, I—I'm just fascinated. All of this could make a great movie or book."

"Yes, it certainly could! However, this is not a profession you want to lose yourself in. I actually wanted to ask if you could lead a counseling session with him next week while I'm out of town. But if it will be too much for you in any way... there is no obligation."

I blinked, my eyes wide with shock.

"You think I'm ready for a session with him?"

"I don't see why not. Considering Jeremy has yet to work on any of the positive thinking strategies I've given him, I figure that will be no problem for you to continue. He will be restrained as an extra measure, if that makes you feel better."

"Um, well—sure. I can handle it."

"Very good. I will have the session arranged for you next Wednesday."

3 - BELIEVE

The machine and alleged murder cover up made me lie awake during the nights that led up to my session with Jeremy. Out of all the different live-ins I could have imagined working with, I never thought a case could so easily intrigue and horrify me.

When Dr. Harris left Mulden-Hale the next week to go out of town, he dropped off his latest session notes with Jeremy—a session I hadn't attended.

My heart pounded while I sat at my desk reviewing them the next day, unsettled to read that Jeremy had had another outburst and left early again.

Can I really handle this... even if he's restrained?

I closed my eyes and took a few deep, steady breaths just like I'd learned during my own time in therapy. Although working with behavioral patients was an important step in my career, it certainly felt daunting. But once a few minutes passed, I managed to gain a better sense of confidence.

Maybe I can reach Jeremy in a way that Dr. Harris can't. I won't get sucked into his delusions.

● ● ● ● ● ●

Jeremy arrived not long after I did to the same room I had observed him in the week before. When the security officer led him to the couch in a straitjacket, I tried to hide my surprise at the extreme method of restraint that had been chosen.

Although I knew straitjackets were still commonly used in mental facilities, I had never seen a patient inside one before, and it had always seemed like an outdated practice until now.

Instead, I expected handcuffs.

"Sit, and do not move," the security officer ordered, then turned to me. "I'll be right outside the door like normal—shout if you need my help."

I smiled a little and nodded once, my gaze lingering on the floor until the therapy room door closed. Afterward, my eyes flashed to Jeremy, who sat frowning as he stared out the window.

I took a deep breath and smiled.

"Hi Jeremy," I said calmly. "You might remember me from last week when I sat in on one of your sessions with Dr. Harris. I'm Dr. Allsion Collins, and I'm substituting for him today."

My heart pounded slightly as I waited for some kind of reaction, but Jeremy continued staring out the window as if I had never spoken. I cleared my throat and glanced down at his file, my gaze sweeping the bullet-point objectives Dr. Harris had written for me.

"It's okay if you haven't been able to work on any of the five strategies to positive thinking Dr. Harris introduced you to," I said slowly. "Maybe it will be easier if we work on one together. What thought bothers you the most?"

I stared at Jeremy as I waited for him to tell me his mother was a murderer or something about Oliver—but no response. I blinked, already feeling at a loss. In all my previous years of counseling, my patients had always been eager to overcome their setbacks through any therapeutic means. But truthfully, I felt like the problem.

Wait a second—I'm acting like Dr. Harris, and Jeremy knows it. I won't reach him if I act like a clone. Maybe all he wants is what I wanted through my trauma...

I sighed and closed his file, deciding to ignore the structure Dr. Harris had laid out for me. If Jeremy could freely talk about his reality and feel believed—which had yet to happen—that could begin his path to healing much faster. And honestly, I wanted to know more, too.

"What was it like inside the machine?"

Jeremy's head snapped in my direction, his eyes wide as the hair on my arms rose.

"It was very bright, and I leaned on a thin metal slab that had leather straps and a footrest. It was made for putting people inside... probably against their will."

I blinked, slightly alarmed though relieved to finally have his attention.

"You said one of the accelerators blasted you with radiation and after that you could hear people's thoughts, or rather, *secrets* for a while. Correct?"

"Yes. I promise I'm not lying—I promise."

"Don't worry about that. But Jeremy... why did you go inside the machine?"

The lively look in his eye suddenly dulled.

"I wanted to impress someone... my coworker. She was trying to fix it."

"Julie Carmichael?"

"Yeah... how do you know?"

"I've seen her name a few times in your file. Does she know about the radiation or what happened to you?"

"Yes, but I quit after the company sold the machine, and I haven't spoken to her since."

"Oh. Does she think you're crazy?"

"No."

"Then why haven't you spoken to her?"

Disappointment settled across his face, and Jeremy looked out the window again. I bit my lip, knowing I needed to keep the momentum going.

"Why do you think the voices stopped after two years?"

"I don't know."

"Well, isn't it great you no longer hear them?"

Jeremy's eyes shifted in my direction, but his head didn't move.

"I used to think my life would be easier if I couldn't hear people's thoughts anymore, but now my life is worse without it."

"What? How so?"

"Do you think a straitjacket is comfortable? If I could tell you your darkest secret, you wouldn't doubt anything I've said that put me in this place."

I furrowed my eyebrows and shook my head.

"That's not necessarily true. What if I don't have a dark secret?"

Jeremy turned his head from the window and blinked, his frown remaining.

"Then you're a waste of time, just like Dr. Harris and everyone else here."

I failed to respond as a wave of anger struck me. Despite trying to engage Jeremy more genuinely, my efforts had gone nowhere, and he seemed determined to outsmart me at any turn.

But he wouldn't win. I would help him, even if it went beyond what was professionally necessary.

I cleared my throat and sat up straighter, letting my anger drain out as I smoothed a few wrinkles in my pants.

"Something horrible happened to me when I was very young, and no one believed my side of the story," I confessed, keeping my tone steady. "While there may not be a way to prove a lot of what you've told us—at least at this present moment—I want you to know that I take your claims seriously, and if it would bring you validation or hope, I will look into the black machine and confirm its existence."

While I tried to look brave despite my anxiety, Jeremy stared at me with increasing shock. I sat rigidly as I waited for him to say something, wondering if I had taken an irreversible step inside the rabbit hole.

"You're not serious."

His quiet voice shook slightly, and I nodded once.

"I am."

Jeremy shifted beneath his straitjacket, his gaze fixated on me.

"No one else should suffer like I have," he said, hushed. "If you find it... don't go inside it, or even touch it. Don't go anywhere near it."

I smiled a little, ignoring the chill along my spine in the suddenly ominous atmosphere.

"I promise I won't," I replied gently. "All I need is a record of it arriving at the medical supply company or it being sold. I'm sure there is a picture documented somewhere in that paperwork as well. And once I have the proof, I'll put it in your file, because I want you to know that I believe in you and your recovery."

Jeremy's gaze fell from mine, and after a few hitched breaths, I saw several tears run down his cheeks.

● ● ● ● ● ●

Later that night, I lay awake on the couch and stared at endless commercials flashing across the TV screen.

After trying to sleep for the last few hours, I couldn't get the image of Jeremy crying out of my head, and all the reasons—both personal and professional—that it tore at my heart. I didn't want to lose myself in my job like Dr. Harris warned, but as I tried to untangle the web of any patient that came my way... it seemed impossible to avoid. And the possible confirmation of the black machine's existence also kept me awake, as I couldn't help but wonder about Jeremy's second claim: that it enabled him to hear dark thoughts.

As crazy as that seemed, I still wanted to believe him.

I rolled onto my back and sighed heavily, wishing my brain had a literal off switch. After I left work earlier, I felt upset at myself for getting sucked in just like Dr. Harris suspected, but now, I didn't care.

One step into the rabbit hole wasn't that far.

If Jeremy lived in the black abyss at the bottom, I was still at the top, bathed in sunlight and hardly inside.

I closed my eyes again and waited for sleep to come.

People called me a liar and my story was much easier to believe... I won't discount him so easily.

4 - DREAM

I left work early Monday afternoon and drove across town to another, though much smaller, mental health facility. The discrete brown brick building had little curb appeal, and once I parked, I walked inside through one of the main glass doors.

I smiled as I checked in with the receptionist, then headed toward my usual room—9A. My pulse raced as I wondered how I might explain Jeremy and the machine, along with my offer to prove its existence in some kind of sane, rational way. Although I had my reason to help him, I didn't particularly want to explain them to anyone else.

I stopped in front of the door to therapy room 9A, sighing to myself before I twisted the knob and entered. It was a small room similar to the therapy rooms at Mulden-Hale, and my therapist—Dr. Bethany Haviland—grinned warmly at me as I settled into the couch across from her. She wore a gray blouse with black pants that day, and her salt and pepper hair laid straight and reached her shoulders. Dr. Haviland's red glasses rested near the tip of her nose, and on her lap was a yellow legal pad.

"Good afternoon, Allison," she said calmly. "I hope all is well lately."

I smiled awkwardly, wishing the last few weeks of my life had been as plain and nearly boring as the months before.

"I suppose it is, except for one thing," I admitted. "But before I get to that, I want to talk about a dream I had last night—one I haven't had in years. This time, it ended differently... it was a lot more terrifying."

Dr. Haviland furrowed her eyebrows while she observed me over the rim of her glasses.

"The dream about the dog attack?"

"Yes, but this time...."

My throat suddenly went dry and ached as tears stung at the corners of my eyes. I quickly grabbed a tissue from the box on the table beside me, though I squeezed it in my hand instead of using it right away.

"Allison, what happened?"

"I did what everyone accused me of years ago... I opened the gate and let the dog out of the fence."

The tears that burned finally fell to my cheeks, but I swiftly wiped them away.

"And right after the dog mauled my legs, I saw everyone in my neighborhood standing around me—including his terrible owner that lied in the first place. But they were all there, pointing at me and yelling while I was all bloody and couldn't even move. I thought I was going to die right there, because I made a mistake and everyone thought I deserved what happened."

I squeezed my eyes shut and pressed the tissue against them, trying to ignore how real the nightmare still felt.

"I'm so sorry, Allison," Dr. Haviland said gently. "There must be something new in your life that triggered this dream and its altered ending. You mentioned there is one thing bothering you?"

"Yes," I replied after a moment, pulling the tissue away. "I started working with my first behavioral patient, and although it's not clear to what degree he is mentally unstable, there is a certain part of his past I agreed to help him with beyond therapy."

"Oh? What is that?"

"He blames a black machine for a lot of his trauma, and well... I said I would research it and put proof of its existence inside his file. Maybe I'm worried about nothing, but no one believes anything he says about what happened to him... and I know what that feels like."

While I wiped away a few more tears, Dr. Haviland crossed her legs and sighed, her expression difficult to read.

"I would not normally recommend diving into a patient's past more than what is professionally required," she replied slowly. "But if you are able without consequence, then perhaps it is necessary for you and your patient on many levels. I believe our dreams can relay important information about ourselves, and it's possible your dream changed to confirm you are doing the right thing."

I blinked a few times while I listened, then released a sigh of relief.

"I think it did," I replied. "But I promise I did not open the gate—I would never do that."

"I know, Allison," Dr. Haviland said sympathetically. "The dog jumped the fence and attacked you."

New tears blurred my vision as I nodded, surprised by how fresh the trauma of that day started to feel again.

"Dogs are powerful creatures," I said, my voice almost desperate. "It was a tall fence but I watched him charge toward me and jump it effortlessly. That dog growled and barked at everyone—not just me. Maybe I should have taken a different route home from the bus like my parents told me to, but that one was the shortest, and I never, not once, even *touched* the fence—"

I stopped abruptly as I found it difficult to breathe and buried my face into a new tissue.

It wasn't right that a twelve-year-old girl should be blamed after getting her legs mauled and nearly bleeding to death. But the man who owned that dog hated my father, and the more I suffered, so did he.

• • • • • •

Later that week, I stopped by a coffee house after work and settled into a table in the back corner. The calm atmosphere paired with a warm latte helped me ease into some overdue relaxation, but I also decided it was time to finally contact Julie Carmichael.

After opening my laptop, I pulled up the website of the medical supply company Jeremy had worked at and typed her name in the search bar. Although I wasn't sure if it would get me anywhere, I felt disappointed when an error message appeared on the next page.

I sighed heavily—already out of ideas.

But after a few long seconds of staring painfully at the white page, I opened a new tab and typed her name and the medical supply company into the internet search bar. To my delight, a professional networking profile was listed within the first five results, and after clicking it, I saw her picture and department title, as well as an email address.

This is her—it has to be.

I dragged my cursor over the email and pasted it into the recipient field of a new email message. Despite my excitement, my mind froze as deciding what to say—or even how to begin—felt impossible. If Jeremy had truly made up the machine, I was going to look ridiculous, or even crazy myself.

But eventually, I began to type.

> *Hi Julie,*
> *I'm a therapist working with your former colleague Jeremy Gregory and I wanted to confirm if a black machine he has talked extensively about is real, and if there are any records of it. I am sorry to bother you and I understand if none of this makes sense. I appreciate any help.*
> *Thank you,*
> *Allison Collins*

My pulse raced while I read the email several times before I finally sent it. Afterward, I took a deep breath and grabbed my latte, which I had almost forgotten about. As I sipped at it, I glanced at the time on my laptop, seeing it was a little past 6:30 p.m.

I didn't have much to return home to other than the TV and a book I was reading, so while I sank into nervous anticipation, I tried to distract myself by window-shopping several websites for clothes and purses. However, not more than a half hour passed before I received a notification of a new email, which nearly caused my heart to palpitate.

Julie Carmichael had responded.

5 - CALL

I stared at the notification in the bottom right corner of the screen as if it might be a hallucination. But when it disappeared a few seconds later, I clicked on the email tab of my internet browser and saw Julie's unread email sitting at the top of the list.

Without another thought, I pressed my finger to the touch pad and clicked on it.

> *Allison,*
> *The machine does exist and I do have paperwork documenting its arrival here and placement into auction. While I cannot release my paperwork, the local auction should have easily accessible public records. I labeled it as a Medical Radiation*

Generator and it was auctioned on May 15th two
years ago. That's all I know.
~ Julie

My jaw dropped after I read her response—the warmth of the sun at the top of the rabbit hole fading as I slipped a few more feet down.

I opened another tab and pulled up the local auction house website, which had an archive page of public records spanning many years. A link for each year was listed neatly in a single column, and I scrolled to the bottom of the page to find the one I needed. But after clicking it, a new column listing each month was displayed, and I selected May, followed by the specific date. I held my breath as a PDF automatically opened, and a few pages in, I saw separate records of each item sold, including the price, buyer, and item details.

The PDF was a little more than one hundred pages, and I tried to stay patient while I began to search for the Medical Radiation Generator—which I found almost a half hour later. It was the forty-sixth record in the document, and my gaze swept over the dimensions, which were certainly large enough to match Jeremy's claims about it.

My heart thudded as I switched back to my email and responded to Julie's message with a request to speak on the phone that evening, or at her earliest convenience to ask a few more questions. Although I half-expected her to turn me down, she wrote back quickly and agreed to a phone call at eight o'clock.

* * * * * *

I sat on my couch later that night waiting for my cell phone to ring. While the minutes wound down to eight o'clock, I hoped Dr. Harris wouldn't be too upset to see the auction record of the machine in Jeremy's file next week, for it laid printed out on my coffee table.

In all the new hire paperwork I'd signed before accepting the job, I never saw a document limiting my range of assistance for patients—though honestly, it was difficult for me to remember everything in the large stack I'd been handed. But whether I had started to break a rule or not, the sudden ringing of my cell phone let me know it was too late to turn back now.

I answered the call and swallowed.

"Hello?"

"Allison? This is Julie."

"Hi! Great—thank you so much for taking the time to call."

"No problem," Julie replied, her voice steady. "How is... Jeremy?"

"He's alright—could be better," I admitted. "But I wanted to find proof of the machine to bring him some validation. I think that will do a lot for his mental health."

"Yes, maybe."

"I won't take much of your time, but Jeremy says the machine made it possible for him to hear other people's thoughts... and he said you believed him. I'm just curious why that is?"

Her end of the line stayed silent, and I bit my lip, hoping I hadn't ruined her willingness to talk.

"You'll probably want to lock me away, too," she finally blurted. "But I do believe it—in fact, I know he heard my thoughts one night."

Julie took a deep breath while I anxiously waited, though also excited.

"I don't tell this to everyone, but since you're a therapist and this is about Jeremy... I don't care. A few weeks after he went inside the machine, we were having dinner at his apartment and talking about the thoughts he heard that day... but later on, he asked me to be his girlfriend. I was shocked because he knew I wasn't looking to date anyone then, but we were hanging out so much after work because of the machine that I guess he couldn't resist. And I... well... I thought of why I didn't want to date him before I said no nicely, and he heard it."

Her breath drew in sharply all of a sudden, and I frowned, listening to her begin to cry.

"I'll never forget how his happiness drained into pure disappointment. I didn't know what to say as I could no longer find a single doubt about his supernatural ability—but Jeremy learned my secret, that I had cheated on my ex-husband for two years before he found out, and that I wouldn't date anyone because I was in the middle of a divorce and going through therapy. I knew Jeremy heard it because he repeated all of it out loud to me, and of course, I told him it was true. He never looked at me the same after that, and he quit a month later without telling me."

I sighed heavily and gave Julie a minute to compose herself, pulling my legs up close to me on the couch.

"Thank you for sharing all this with me," I said softly at length. "You've given me a lot to think about, and now I can help Jeremy better."

"Good," Julie replied, her tone less upset. "There's no way he could have easily found all that out, and because of that night... I believe everything he's told me about his mother, too. But his family turned against him, and the fact that he can't prove her confession is probably what drove him mad."

This time, I could hardly speak as her knowledge of the alleged murder caught me by surprise, but it soon made perfect sense that she would know.

"Oh, right, yes—that's been another piece of this puzzle," I replied, stupefied.

"There's something else I should mention in case it's important. When I was working on the machine, I found out that it produced Macro-molecule radiation, and started researching that online. I didn't find anything except an old college paper theorizing about it and its effects, and to me it seemed like the person who wrote it also had to invent that machine. The author of the paper is Paul Henderson if you want to look him up."

"What? Who?"

"Paul Henderson."

My eyes widened as I suddenly felt short of breath, my gaze eventually shifting to the auction record lying on my coffee table.

A chill ran down my spine as I could no longer see or feel the light at the top of the rabbit hole, but had abruptly stumbled into darkness.

"I can't believe it, Julie—it's actually very important that you mentioned it. If Paul did create the machine... then the auction record states that he's the one who bought it back."

6 - CARTER

Later that night, I sat in bed with my laptop in front of me while reading Paul's old college paper. It turned up easily in the search results after typing in his name and Macro-molecule radiation—which he spent over thirty pages theorizing how it could alter the appearance and function of any living organism if produced.

But eight years had passed since he wrote it, and I had the evidence he had figured it out by way of a mysterious black machine.

I sighed and took a break from reading as my mind wandered past Jeremy into the possibility of other people—or victims—also affected by Paul's altering machine. But the number seemed impossible to guess without knowing how long his invention had been in existence.

Jeremy went inside it willingly... was Paul able to convince anyone himself?

I bit my lip as I tried to imagine the machine I had proof of actually being real—and how it could erase the ugly scars on my legs that I spent so many years hiding.

No, I don't care about it anymore... I would never go inside that machine.

The temptation faded as I opened a new browser tab and typed in Paul's name by itself, hoping to find a picture or any more information on him. But when the results loaded, I saw dozens of men across the country with the same name, and I felt deflated.

A minute later, I tried something else: *black machine macro radiation.*

I held my breath but nothing appeared—not even Paul's college paper. Frustrated, I started trying several variations, until I suddenly received a page of results with the phrase: *black machine DNA.*

The first six links were for medical equipment for DNA lab analysis, but the seventh link directed to a post on an online forum. My eyes widened as I quickly clicked it, entering a website with a chat board titled: STRANGE AND UNTIMELY DEATH STORIES.

A long post by a registered user filled the page, and I could hardly believe what I read as my gaze swept over the text:

Hey, everyone. It makes me sad to see that so many people have lost friends and loved ones in weird ways—usually without a lot of answers—and unfortunately I have my own story to tell. You'll probably think it's fake, but remember what thread we're in after all. It's not going to make total sense or seem real—it still doesn't to me.

Anyway, one of my best childhood friends went missing last summer. We weren't as close then as we were years ago, but still kept in touch now and again. I hadn't heard from her in a few months when I found out she had recently been reported missing on the news and I immediately contacted her family, who told me she hadn't come back from a trip to Lake Tahoe a few days earlier.

She was only twenty-three and to this day, not I or anyone else knows what happened to her. But here is the strangest part. Almost three weeks after her disappearance, I received a letter from someone claiming to be her! In it the person told me that she was safe again with her family, but that she couldn't tell anyone or see me because she had been put inside a black machine that entirely changed her DNA and how she looked. (Still reading?)

She said I had always been a great friend and that she wanted me to know she would be okay. I was really disturbed by this letter and hated to think that someone—who had to be close to all of us—would mess with me like that. I've never said a word about it to her family for obvious reasons, but my friend's name was Dana Carter, and you can find articles...

My stomach twisted and I stopped reading as my thoughts became paralyzed with shock. But after a moment, I searched the name DANA CARTER, which yielded several pages of articles about her disappearance that occurred almost an hour from where I lived in Reno.

In the first article, I learned that she disappeared on July 12th almost three years ago after an honors club retreat with her college peers. Authorities had estimated that she disappeared at some point after leaving Lake Tahoe, for she never returned to her college campus, and neither she, her car, or belongings were found.

My pulse raced as I struggled to believe what I wondered about earlier—that there were *more* victims besides Jeremy, and Dana had possibly ended up even less fortunate. I clicked back to the chat board post and read it again, wishing by the end that I could believe the letter was a hoax. But the rabbit hole was too dark now, and the only way out seemed to be forward.

If all of this is true and Dana really sent the letter herself, then... did Paul kidnap and release her? Or did she escape? Who is Paul really and what's going on?

My gaze shifted to the username of the poster—HawaiiSun089—and I clicked into their profile, seeing the person was listed as female and marked her location as Nevada. But my heart skipped a beat when I noticed the most recent post on her account had been made over a year ago. Although a MESSAGE ME button sat beneath her profile photo of a tabby cat, I doubted it would do much good. For a few minutes I debated contacting her, but finally gave into the urge.

Once I set up my own account, I typed a private message, then closed my laptop for the night.

> *Hi HawaiiSun089,*
> *I'm so sorry you lost your friend! I believe Dana*
> *Carter may have sent you that letter, because I*
> *know another person who said they went inside*
> *a black machine that changed them. I have also*
> *confirmed this story with an eye witness and*
> *auction records that describe the machine in*
> *detail. If this message reaches you, I'm very eager*

to talk more. Maybe we can unravel the truth of what's going on together?

• • • • • •

After my morning sessions the next day, I finally made my way to Dr. Harris's office. I hoped he would let me see Jeremy again—whether it was through our own private session or another sit-in—and I could easily imagine the excitement on Jeremy's face when I told him about the auction records, though I hadn't decided if I would mention the post on the chat board yet.

When I reached Dr. Harris's office, I quickly knocked on the door, though he answered only after a minute of silence. His gloomy expression troubled me, and I tried to smile politely despite my bad timing.

"Good morning," I said softly. "When you have a minute, I would like to talk about Jeremy. But I understand if now is not a good time."

Dr. Harris sighed heavily, and to my surprise, he motioned me forward with his hand.

"It is a bad time, but also an appropriate one to discuss Jeremy. Come in, Allison."

My heart sank as I followed him into the office and gently closed the door behind me. The room was slightly larger than my office, and instead of a couch along the wall opposite of his desk, he had a bookshelf and two cushioned chairs with a small table between them. Dr. Harris strode over to the chair closest to the bookcase and sat down, and I quickly occupied the empty one near it.

"What's wrong with him?" I asked, unable to contain my worry any longer.

"Well, his doctor called me about his MRI results this morning," Dr. Harris replied, his gaze cast down on the carpet. "And as it turns out... Jeremy has fatal brain lesions."

I gasped as my blood began to race, hardly knowing if I could believe a single word he said.

"Is the doctor sure it's terminal?"

"Yes, he is quite sure. The lesions are across Jeremy's frontal lobe, and based on similar cases, his doctor told me he will soon lose the ability to function normally before he falls unconscious and passes away."

"How did this happen?"

"The cause hasn't been determined, which is frustrating."

"Does Jeremy know?"

"No... I haven't told him yet, but I will this afternoon."

I sighed heavily and leaned back into the chair with tears stinging at the corner of my eyes.

"Do you think I could see him again?"

"Sure—I'm glad your counseling session with him went well while I was away. I can arrange something for you tomorrow."

I smiled and wiped a stray tear on my cheek.

"Thank you."

● ● ● ● ● ●

Jeremy already sat waiting in the therapy room when I entered the next afternoon. All the joy I felt about my research into the black machine had practically vanished, and I only looked at him after sitting down across from the couch and making myself comfortable.

Jeremy stared out the nearby window with a resigned expression, as though he were disappointed but not entirely surprised. But at least, I was glad to see that he had no form of restraint on him.

"Good afternoon," I said quietly, and slightly awkwardly. "I'm glad Dr. Harris let me have another session with you, because I want to say I'm sorry about the recent changes in your health... but I've also looked into the machine, and found evidence of it."

Jeremy slowly turned his head toward me, but he didn't say anything. I smiled a little and opened the folder on my lap, pulling out a copy of the auction record.

"Here it is," I said, my voice increasingly eager. "I spoke to Julie like you suggested, and I couldn't have found it without her."

I stood up and placed the auction record on his lap, and Jeremy picked it up, carefully studying it.

"How are you feeling?" I asked.

"Better now," Jeremy replied at length. "I guess I will die in the same way my brother should have."

I frowned and sighed.

"Dr. Harris told me the doctor isn't sure why you developed the lesions... but I've been wondering if it had something to do with the machine."

"Probably. That thing is cursed, and the radiation it creates is strange."

"But why now? Why not right away?"

Jeremy shrugged, his demeanor having an air of defeat.

"Julie also told me about the college paper written by Paul Henderson, which theorizes about the Macro-molecule radiation," I said, changing the subject. "It could be capable of all kinds of things, and I have no doubt Paul built the machine. But if you look at the auction record... it appears he bought it back. There is no address listed, though."

Jeremy blinked as his eyes widened, and he quickly double-checked the auction record before meeting my gaze again.

"I've never met the guy, obviously, but he has to be crazy," he said, almost afraid. "Who builds a machine like that? It's designed to trap people and experiment on them."

I nodded, my expression grim.

"I wouldn't doubt it. But I want you to know that I believe you, and now there is a reason for everyone else to believe you too."

"What about my parents?" Jeremy asked suddenly. "Do you believe my mother watched my younger brother drown? I'm not lying when I say she confessed it, but there's no way to prove it."

"Yes, I believe that too," I said, my voice almost a whisper. "And I wish something could be done about that. But Jeremy..."

My gaze dropped from his face to my lap as I hesitated, wondering if it was worthwhile to share my story. But a strong urge in my gut quickly convinced me it was necessary.

"I know what it's like not to be believed—that's one of the reasons I wanted to help you," I confessed. "When I was younger, a dog mauled me on my way home from school, and the man who owned it claimed that I let the dog out of the fence, which I would never, *ever* do. But my father called the cops on him earlier that summer when his brush pile fire got out of control, and he hated my dad ever since. But everyone in the neighborhood believed his lie—that I had let the dog out, and no one seemed to care at all about my suffering."

Jeremy furrowed his eyebrows and stared at me intensely, though he said nothing. I sighed and shrugged, trying to stay calm while I ignored a wave of strong emotions.

"I have scars all over my legs because of it, and we moved from Washington to Nevada a year later. I spent many years in therapy to heal from what happened," I continued. "But no matter what happens to you, I wanted you to know why I cared about helping. Anyway, there is something else about the machine that I'm trying to look into."

"What is it?"

"I found a post written by someone on a chat board describing the strange disappearance of her friend, and how she received a letter one day from that person—Dana Carter—telling her she was safe but could not see her because her entire appearance had been changed inside a DNA-altering machine! I could hardly believe what I was reading, and I sent the woman a message for more details, but I have no idea if she'll respond."

Jeremy blinked, his mouth falling open slightly.

"Seriously? How long ago was the post written?"

"Almost three years ago, and the woman who wrote it hasn't been active in over a year. I figure I still have a good chance of reaching her if she gets email notifications from the site."

Jeremy nodded, his expression bewildered until he looked at me more seriously.

"Thank you for telling me about your scars and the dog. I believe it jumped the fence, just like you said. Before Oliver died, we had a dog that could jump our seven-foot fence, and we found him dead in the street one day after being hit by a car."

I gasped as my eyes widened, experiencing a fresh flood of validation.

"I don't know how tall that man's fence was, but it was high," I replied. "If I hadn't seen the dog jump it myself, I might not believe it either. Thank you, Jeremy—I knew I wasn't crazy."

He smiled a little and nodded.

"I definitely understand how strange things happen that no one can explain. My diagnosis doesn't give me much time, but what you've done means so much to me. I hardly feel ready to die, but since you've taken me seriously, it does make it a lot easier."

Jeremy's face started to turn red, and as he fought back tears, I tried to resist my own and failed.

"Is there anything else I can do for you?" I asked, struggling to keep my voice steady.

"Yeah," Jeremy said, wiping his eyes with his sleeve. "If you're ever able to stop this from happening to someone else, please do it. I don't care how."

I smiled a little, despite doubting I could do much more than I already had.

"Okay. I promise."

7 - PICTURE

Three days after seeing Jeremy, I received an email that HawaiiSun089 had replied to my message. I could hardly believe it as I logged into my account from my couch, almost having convinced myself it was too late to contact her.

As my eyes poured over her response, my bewilderment only grew:

Hi Blueberries_3,

I'm sorry I didn't get back to you sooner—I'm not good with email and haven't logged in for quite some time. But I'm really surprised the machine is real and you think the letter is too. I still don't know what to make of it, but there is something I didn't mention.

The person who sent the letter also included a picture of a young woman, but I have no idea who she is and I've tried searching the internet for face matches, however, no luck. She's very beautiful and I'm assuming that it's supposed to be a picture of Dana, since the letter claimed a machine changed how she looked. It's all really wild and I thought mentioning it in the forum would make my story even more unbelievable. But I'm not lying whatsoever (see attached image).

I'm glad you've done further research into this to gather proof, but I still don't know what to believe since Dana's family has never contacted me to confirm she returned to them in any fashion, and like I said, I wasn't going to bother them with this twilight zone stuff. My friend is still listed as a missing person and I know I will always hope for the best for her, whatever that is now.

~ Bree a.k.a HawaiiSun089

I clicked the image link and a picture appeared, showing the face of a stunning young woman. She sat on the floor near a bed and looked into the camera with a slight frown. Her blue eyes and red lips looked striking within her pale complexion, and her glossy brown hair laid in a thick braid over her shoulder.

I could tell she snapped the picture herself because of the slight tilted angle and one of her arms being outstretched. After saving the picture to my computer, I opened another tab and searched for a real picture of Dana Carter—or at least, the one that the world knew. The differences between the two women were extreme, and if the letter and picture were a hoax, I couldn't imagine what someone had to gain from the effort.

I switched back to my chat board account and wrote back to Bree, thanking her for sharing the photo and that I would keep her posted of any further developments. Afterward, I clicked back to the news article with Dana's verified photo, remembering her parents lived only an hour south of me.

But when a brief thought about researching their address crossed my mind... I blushed and shook my head.

This is it—this is where the rabbit hole ends. I cannot possibly bother these people who lost their daughter with all of this, even if it's real...

I sighed heavily and pressed my hand to my forehead, wondering if I needed more help than Dr. Haviland could give.

●　●　●　●　●　●

The lesions acted swiftly. Three weeks after Jeremy was diagnosed, a patient attendant found him passed away in his bed one morning.

I could hardly look at Dr. Harris in the month that followed, for I could tell Jeremy's death weighed heavily on him, and it didn't take much to bring me to tears either. But I did cry in private, and chose not to attend his funeral as the uncomfortable presence of his parents would make it even more difficult.

And despite my decision to end my research into the machine, the idea that Bree's photo *was* Dana and that she could still be alive nagged at me. Although I truly started to feel crazy, it made sense that Dana's family might not report her return if she looked nothing like the girl in the news article photos anymore.

When another month passed and I still couldn't let it go, I knew I had to fall deeper, and unravel the letter of Dana's story.

●　●　●　●　●　●

Saturday morning, I plugged the address of the Carter residence into the navigation screen of my car after settling down in the driver's seat. Their home address had been easy to find in an online person directory of the city where they lived, and the drive would be roughly forty minutes.

I felt half insane as I started the drive, wondering how terrible of a person I might be if the Carter family did not take me seriously. But, I didn't have to dump my whole theory on them at once—I could simply ask if Dana ever returned home under strange circumstances, and if it were true or they wanted to know more, then I could share everything I had managed to piece together. Whether this approach was great or not, it gave me enough comfort to keep my foot on the pedal.

Almost ten minutes into the drive, I finally turned onto the highway, slightly distracted from my anxiety by a woman's lifestyle podcast. The episode had a panel of women discussing what it was like to date men from different professions, and I smiled when one of them dove into her prior relationship with a police officer. If everything went well with the Carters... I had an even crazier idea I could reach out to *Liam* about, which could bring us closer together in an effort to end this unimaginable terror for good.

Thirty minutes later, I drove slowly down the road that led to the Carter house, eyeing each house number on the mailboxes I passed. And a few minutes later, I turned into the driveway of an old white house with a wide front porch. A red SUV sat beside the house at the end of a long driveway, and I felt relieved that *someone* was home without knowing their schedule.

I parked a comfortable distance away from the red SUV and climbed out of my car with my heart pounding. My hair was pulled into a ponytail and I wore blue jeans with a pink shirt that had short lace sleeves—my unspoken effort to look nice and normal before everything took a wild turn.

My feet felt like lead as I climbed the porch steps and approached the front door, pulling back the screen and quickly knocking. I concentrated on taking deep, even breaths until the door finally opened, and I saw an older, heavy-set woman in a casual summer dress in front of me. Her short hair lay straight around her head, and her make up was minimal.

I smiled both awkwardly and politely.

"Hi," I said, extending my hand. "I'm Allison Collins, a therapist and psychologist at Mulden-Hale mental health facility in Reno. I've come to ask a question about your daughter Dana, if that's okay? But if this is not a good time, please let me know. "

To my relief, she smiled and shook my hand.

"Sure, I don't mind. I'm Sandra Carter, Dana's mother as you may know. Did you know her?"

"No, but I recently spoke to someone who did, and that conversation brought me here today. Please forgive me, but... is it possible Dana returned home, and under strange circumstances?"

Sandra blinked, suddenly shaking her head.

"What? I haven't seen my daughter since her disappearance years ago."

The heat of embarrassment rose across my entire body as I smashed into rocks at the bottom of the rabbit hole, wishing I had kept my decision to give it all up and resurface.

"Of course—I'm so sorry! I spoke to her long time friend Bree, and she said someone might have played a hoax on her about Dana and a black machine not long after she was reported missing. But that's settled now and I won't waste your time any longer. Have a good—"

"A black machine?"

Sandra slowly raised an eyebrow as her expression turned grave.

"Um, yes—crazy, right?"

"Allison, please come inside."

● ● ● ● ● ●

I sat at the dining room table and tried to contain my curiosity while Sandra put on a pot of coffee nearby in the kitchen. After pressing the start button on the coffee machine, she opened the cabinet above it and took out two mismatched mugs.

"Do you want cream and sugar?"

I nodded, smiling.

"Yes—thank you."

Sandra grabbed a clear glass jar half-full of sugar from the same cabinet as the mugs, then walked to the fridge and removed a small carton of half-and-half. When she brought these to the table, she sat down in the chair across from me, her expression difficult to read.

"Please tell me about this hoax," she said. "I'm glad to learn anything concerning my daughter."

"Sure," I said, trying to sound casual. "I found Bree through an online chat board where she wrote a post saying she was friends with Dana and after she disappeared, she received a strange letter that claimed to be from Dana and included a picture, but it looked nothing like her. The letter writer said she was safe with her family again but that she couldn't see Bree or anyone else because a black machine had changed her appearance."

My gaze fell from Sandra's to the table top, unsure how she might respond to such a story.

"Yes," she said, after a quiet moment. "I remember that letter."

I looked at her immediately in shock, my mouth falling open a little. But before I could respond, Sandra stood and went to the coffee maker, pouring us each a cup before she set one in front of me and sat down again.

"You know about it?" I said, bewildered. "It's not a sick joke?"

"Oh, no," she replied, shaking her head as she poured creamer into her cup. "Dana and I talked about it, and we agreed it would be fine to try to let Bree know everything would be alright—at least for a little while—even if she never believed it. I'm sorry I lied about not seeing Dana since her disappearance, but I'm still struggling to understand the true story of what happened to her. However, the girl in that photo *is* my daughter. She had every memory to prove it."

Numbly, I reached for the creamer and sugar, slowly preparing my coffee as I felt unexpectedly lifted and restored to life from the rocks.

"This is so incredible," I finally blurted. "Where is Dana now?"

Sandra drew in a deep, heavy breath, her gaze lingering on her coffee cup.

"Why did you come here?" she asked, her tone quiet and sad. "Surely you don't go chasing down the truth to every wild story you read online."

"No, I don't," I replied. "But a patient of mine just died and he claimed to have been in that black machine too. He wasn't affected the same way, though, and lived for two years after that experience before passing on recently. I actually looked into the validity of such a machine for him—to bring him some validation and solace if I could—and discovered that it is real. There's an eye-witness to the whole event, and I found auction records that describe it just like he did."

Sandra's gaze widened while I spoke, and by the end, her hand lay across her chest, her face switching between surprise and horror.

"Dana is dead, too. We had her with us for a month before she passed. She said the machine damaged her bone marrow, and that she couldn't live for very long without a special powder her captor made. It was one of many things I struggled to believe, but her health quickly went downhill. In her final days, she had bad nose bleeds and started to cough up blood. She and I would walk to a special place in the woods out back that she had always loved, and she told me to bury her there when she died. That's exactly what her father and I did, and there was no point in a normal funeral—not when no one would recognize her, or believe who she was."

Sandra sighed as her face grew red, and I could see tears along the rim of her eyes. I hardly knew what to think as her story sunk in, filling me with a deep sense of loss and bittersweet respect for Dana's last request.

"Thank you for letting me know—I'm glad she managed to have some measure of peace and happiness. The name of her captor is Paul Henderson. His name is on the auction record, but more importantly, a college paper of his is online theorizing about the special kind of radiation the machine uses to alter people. He has to be the creator of it and the one behind all of this."

Sandra nodded and wiped away a few stray tears from her cheek.

"He is to blame—Dana told me about him. But he was investigated, and there is no evidence."

"What? Are you serious?"

"Yes. Before she returned home, she told the police about what happened to her and where to find him, but he had a clever story, and they did not believe the machine could do anything she said. His house has since burnt down, however. Perhaps he did it to permanently cover his tracks."

"What was his address? Do you remember?"

Sandra nodded, and I slid my cell phone out of my pocket and opened a new note. When she told me, I quickly typed it in.

"Did she say what he looked like?"

"Yes—tall, skinny, and with dirty blond hair. He wore large glasses, too. But you should know that Dana mentioned another girl Paul had transformed as well—a girl named Becky. I suppose you can look into information about her if you want, though I don't know what can be done with any of it. What's happened is too bizarre and there's no hard evidence."

My heart raced at the mention of a *third* victim, and I stood from the chair, my coffee just barely sipped.

"I certainly want to look into Becky," I told Sandra confidently. "I promised my former patient, Jeremy, that I would stop this madness if I could, and while I don't know if I can... I keep finding new information that pushes me forward. I'll keep you updated if there is another big breakthrough. Thank you so much for your hospitality today."

Sandra smiled and nodded, looking less upset while we left the dining room and walked back to the front door.

8 - PLAN

I drove to a small restaurant not far from the Carter's house and chose a booth by the window. The heat of the sun felt good across my skin while I read the menu, and once my waiter arrived, I ordered an iced tea and chicken salad. Afterward, I dialed the Reno police station on my cell phone and hoped to get a hold of Liam. The receptionist greeted me after a few rings, then transferred me to his desk phone.

I tried not to get too excited while I waited for him to answer, but when I got his voicemail, I sighed and left a message with my number.

Just be patient...

But it seemed impossible.

I stared out the window anxiously until the waiter brought my food almost ten minutes later. Fortunately, my delicious salad distracted me for a bit, and when it was almost gone, my cell phone rang. I snatched it from the table and immediately answered the unknown number.

"Hello?"

"Hey—Allison? It's Liam."

"Oh, hi. Thanks for returning my call."

"No problem. What's up?"

"Well, I've kind of gotten myself stuck in the middle of something really strange and I have a question. If someone confessed to kidnapping or murdering another person but there is no body or strong evidence, would that person still go to jail?"

"It's possible. What's your confession?"

I rolled my eyes and laughed.

"I have no confession, I promise. But... I want to get one."

"What?" Liam replied, his easy-going tone vanishing. "What are you involved in?"

I sighed heavily.

"It's a really weird, long story. But if I can find a man named Paul Henderson, I think I know how to get him to confess to kidnapping and murdering Dana Carter. She's a college girl who went missing around Carson City a few years ago."

Liam didn't immediately respond and I heard him typing, then silence.

"I just pulled her file in the database," he finally said. "The last update was from a detective named Rob Shaw, and it looks like they did search Paul's house but found no evidence of a crime. He also stated another woman was claiming to be Dana and accused Paul of the kidnapping."

I furrowed my eyebrows and frowned.

"What other woman?"

"I'm not sure. Shaw wrote that she was never identified and that she left the hospital before they could take her to Mulden-Hale for a psychiatric evaluation."

Blinking, I tried to make sense of this unexpected twist. But when the truth about the mysterious woman struck, I decided to spare Liam the details—at least for now.

"Even if no evidence was found at Paul's house, that doesn't mean he's innocent, and did you know his house has since burned to the ground? That's a bit convenient. If I can get a confession from him, I hope that will be enough to solve the case. And he might also be linked to another disappearance in the area of a girl named Becky."

"Hmm, Becky Johnson?" Liam asked. "I remember seeing her all over the news a few years ago whenever I was in Carson City. Her parents begged for information but I don't think any was ever brought forward."

"We need to dive deeper into this, then. Can you look up a forwarding address for me? It might lead to where Paul is now after his house burned."

Liam agreed, and once I told him the original address, he quickly traced the new one in the database.

"Well, looks like we got him! That address forwards to another in his name in Tuscarora, which is a really small town. It's almost five hours from Reno and a pretty good place to get away from the public. I made an arrest there once."

My mouth spread into a wide grin while my heart pounded.

"We have to go then! I don't care that it's so far away—just hook me up to a wire and I'll get the confession."

"Oh yeah?" Liam replied with a chuckle. "Slow down. What makes you think you can crack a killer?"

"Believe me when I say that *explanation* is best saved for the long drive," I responded. "But will you help me, Liam? I'm entirely serious about this, and I can't do it without backup. I don't work during the weekends, and I can wait until the time is right for you to go."

A short silence passed on his end, and I imagined he was carefully thinking it over.

"I can do it in two weeks," he replied at length. "Is that alright?"

"Absolutely! Thank you."

"No problem. There's a nice diner about halfway there we can grab lunch at, if you want."

"Of course. I'd love to have lunch."

"Great, I'll save your number. See you then."

After the call ended, I leaned back in my booth and struggled to think straight. Although my plan to find and expose Paul was delightfully coming together... the hair on the back of my neck rose as I imagined the moment I finally stood before him, his cold eyes peering into mine.

• • • • • •

On a Sunday morning two weeks later, Liam and I met at a coffee shop downtown at 6 AM. I left my vehicle in the parking lot and climbed into his unassuming gray SUV that would take us all the way to Tuscarora.

Thankfully, Liam was in his normal good spirits and really didn't seem to mind the long trip ahead of us, like I worried he might be by the time it came around. But I easily suspected he enjoyed my company more than a friendly acquaintance, and although I felt the same, I could only focus on the incredible task at hand.

"So, what's the master plan?" he asked as we headed for the highway. "You wanted to save it for the drive, and now I can't wait any longer."

I smiled and looked at him, charmed by his combed hair, black t-shirt and dark wash jeans. That day, I'd chosen a green scoop neck tee with light gray sweatpants and tennis shoes.

"Well, in order to explain my master plan, I have to tell you a few things you might find hard to believe."

Liam took a sip of his coffee and glanced at me with a brow raised.

"Go for it, Allison. You wouldn't believe what I have to deal with on a daily basis in my line of work."

"Okay—but don't say I didn't warn you."

As we turned right onto a highway ramp, I started leading Liam into the rabbit hole—from my first session with Jeremy all the way to my promise to him, and ultimately my meeting with Sandra Carter after discovering Dana's story through the online chat board. It took me almost a half hour to get through it all, and the whole time, I waited for Liam to show some sign that he thought our whole mission was nuts. But Liam's face remained cool and collected, and when I finished, he finally looked thoughtful.

"An evil genius terrorizing people with a black machine..." he said after a moment. "That's out there, and I can't believe you spoke to a witness and have an auction record. I've had less evidence for a lot more common crimes. But I guess we'll get to the bottom of it today, won't we? The machine has to be in Tuscarora with Paul."

"Exactly," I replied, relieved. "I'm almost positive his new house has a basement for him to keep it in. And once he's arrested, it needs to be thoroughly inspected."

"Sure, but we need that confession first. How will you get it?"

I bit my lip as my gaze dropped from the highway to my lap. Despite years of therapy helping me find peace with my scars, I suddenly felt hesitant to reveal them to Liam. He could very well find them ugly or repulsive, and I didn't want to lose his promising affections so fast. But—as I had learned with many things in life—his reaction was beyond my control.

I took a deep breath and shrugged.

"I'll just tell him I've heard about what the machine can do, and that I want to go inside it," I said, telling a half-truth and hating my cowardliness. "I'm sure he'll say something incriminating that we can use to arrest him after that, or I'll find another way to coax it out of him."

"Alright. What if he denies everything?"

"I'm not sure, but after all he's done, I don't see why he would—not when I'm hand-delivering myself."

"That *could* make him suspicious of you."

"Maybe. But we have to try, right?"

"Certainly. Criminals deny their crimes all the time, but it doesn't matter with the right evidence."

"Where is the wire equipment?" I asked.

"In a small case behind my seat. I'll get you hooked up when we find a place to park and stake out his house. My gun is also back there."

"Oh—right. Will you come in as soon as you hear the confession?"

"Yeah, or if the situation turns dangerous. I've broken down a few doors before, so don't worry—I can get to you pretty fast."

A small smile turned the corner of my mouth as I looked out the window, imagining myself comforted in his arms after a sudden rescue. But hopefully... my encounter with Paul wouldn't come to that.

9 - TUSCARORA

Around noon that day, Liam and I finally turned into the small town of Tuscarora. It had less than ten public buildings, and as we passed the post office, I felt as though I could see at least one part of every house that populated it, which seemed to only be about twenty-five homes. The sleepy town sat surrounded by miles of open land that eventually led to distant mountains, and its inhabitants seemed to live comfortably in its ramshackle condition.

But I paid less attention to its rustic nature when my pulse started to race as we neared Paul's house, which sat a block from the post office and had no close neighbors. It was a small, dirty white house with two dormer windows and a closed attached garage. A faded blue cargo van sat in front of the garage door, and by looks alone, I couldn't tell whether he was home or not. But in such a small town so far from anywhere else—there were only so many places he could be.

Liam stared out my window as well at the house as we passed it, then he turned the corner to circle the block.

"Let's stakeout at the post office," he said, his tone serious. "We'll get you hooked up and then you can knock on the front door and see if he's home. People in a place like this hardly leave, and they aren't gone for long."

I nodded, my heart pounding in my chest.

"Sure—that sounds good."

When we reached the post office a few minutes later, Liam parked facing the street, and I didn't think our stakeout looked too obvious. Paul's house, though easily in view, would be about a two minute walk from where we were. I sat still as Liam reached behind his seat and pulled a small black case onto this lap. He flipped the latches upward with his thumbs and lifted the top, revealing a small, round microphone with a clip and a palm-sized transmitter lying on top of black foam.

"Clip this under your shirt near your throat," he said, holding the small microphone. "It's powered by a battery that will activate when I turn on the transmitter. Anything you or Paul say will be recorded and come through the transmitter speaker loud and clear."

I smiled, my nerves slightly relaxing.

"Good! I don't want to be in there that long, so the moment he admits the machine killed Dana or Becky, please come bursting in."

"Of course," Liam said with a grin. "I took this job for a reason, and busting in is one of the best parts."

My smile remained as I closed my eyes and took a deep breath. Liam was ready, and well—I had to be ready now. The plan I had formed for the confession felt solid, though if it failed, I would happily excuse myself like an idiot and never return to this town.

● ● ● ● ● ●

The white front door of Paul's house looked even dirtier than the old siding alongside it that was broken in some spots. I stared at the door for a few long seconds before I finally lifted my hand and knocked with decent force.

It was entirely possible that Paul wasn't home, or that he simply wouldn't answer. But Liam and I were determined, and we had decided to wait and try all afternoon if that was what it took. I inhaled deeply while I waited for a response, gently rubbing at the microphone beneath the collar of my shirt, for it itched my skin a little. However, the next few minutes passed with only silence, and I wasn't sure if I should knock again.

He's not here... I should go back to Liam.

I started to turn but stopped, unable to take my eyes off the door as a strange feeling compelled me toward it. I lifted my hand numbly and knocked again, though much harder this time.

"Come on, Paul—open up," I muttered angrily.

The white door remained undisturbed, until I heard a faint *click* on the other side a moment later. Adrenaline shot through my body as the door suddenly opened an inch, revealing nothing but a slice of darkness on the other side. I hardly knew what to think as the gap widened and a face appeared—a face I had tried to conjure only seconds ago, and that I knew existed in the lair at the very end of the long and winding rabbit hole.

Paul—with his pale face, dirty blond hair and glasses—stared at me with little emotion, his eyes squinting from the sunlight. I made a strange sound when I failed to speak, but the door fell back further, allowing me to see the white tank top and light blue denim overalls he wore. Despite a sudden rush of shock and relief, I forced myself to ignore it and begin the plan.

"Hi—I need your help, please," I said, helplessly and innocently. "Do you mind if I come in?"

Paul stared at me and blinked, then stepped aside.

"No... please, come in."

I took note of his calm, husky voice before I stepped inside, trying not to worry if I would make it back out. When he closed the door behind me, my eyes needed a minute to adjust to the dim space. I stood inside a living room that had a couch, sofa chair and TV, and its two windows were mostly covered by thick curtains. The white walls looked dull and slightly yellow, and the chipped wood floor creaked under my feet.

I tried to stay calm as I heard Paul move behind me, though he soon walked in front of me. I smiled awkwardly as I took a moment to study him and felt briefly curious about what he had been doing since the TV wasn't on. Paul seemed content just to stare at me, but I was prepared to lead the conversation anyhow.

"Thank you for letting me in—it's important that we talk. I'm Allison, and you're Paul Henderson, right?"

He nodded slowly.

"Yes."

"Okay, good. I mean, I had an idea of what you looked like, so I figured it was you. But, I came here because I was good friends with Dana Carter, and after seeing what you did to her, *I* want to be changed too."

Paul's eyes widened behind his glasses in the silence; his surprise being the first clear sign of emotion I had noticed. Reaching down, I easily pulled up one side of my sweats, revealing a scarred leg to him.

"See? I want to get rid of these and be a lot more beautiful in other ways, too. You still have it, don't you? The altering machine?"

"Yes... it exists. Please wait here."

Paul then turned from me, and I watched with a stab of genuine concern as he walked toward a staircase resting several feet back from the front door. I fought the urge to abandon my plan and run as he climbed the staircase and disappeared, though I heard a door shut soon after he was out of view.

Inhaling deeply, I bit my lip.

There's no need to panic, but... what is *he doing?*

Minutes passed, and other than a few quiet creaks of the floor, I heard or knew nothing of why he'd gone upstairs. But my suspense faded when Paul returned, taking slow, heavy steps back down into the living room. I hid my suspicion once I quickly looked him over for any kind of change, but found none.

When Paul stood in front of me again, I sensed he might want to say something and waited.

"How is Dana?" he asked, slightly curious.

"Well, she—she passed away. But she told me as long as I took a special powder you made, I would be fine. Is that true?"

Paul nodded.

"So... I'm going to be dosed with radiation? Is that how it works?"

"Yes, but it will be painless. Follow me into the basement. The machine is ready."

A chill shot down my spine as I imagined doing such a thing, but before I could speak, a door upstairs abruptly shut. I flinched, blankly staring at Paul as I wondered if I had actually heard the sound. But his expression stayed cool like ice, and I realized I needed to keep my plan moving.

"Wait—did you know the machine would hurt Dana, or kill her?"

"Yes, I knew. But she could have stayed with me and lived. She chose not to."

Bingo!

"Do I have to stay with you then?"

"No. Dana was... different."

I blinked, sensing his lie in my gut. But this was all part of a plan.

"Okay. I really just want to get rid of these scars. Let's go to the basement."

Paul turned without a word and started walking toward another room beyond an archway. My heart pounded heavily as I slowly followed him, ready for Liam to bust through the front door at any moment. I passed into the next room, which was a small kitchen, and saw the basement door to my right. It stood on the other end of the kitchen, and seemed positioned beneath the living room staircase. When Paul opened the brown door, I had no choice but to walk toward him, trying to hide my surge of anxiety.

Liam, where are you?

Paul's eyes looked oddly empty while his gaze rested on me, and at the open door, I stopped and stared down into darkness.

"Isn't there a light?"

"Yes, of course."

Paul reached into the stairway and flipped a switch on the wall, suddenly illuminating the bottom of the basement. My thoughts raced as I tried to find another excuse to delay our descent, but Paul's hand gripped my wrist in a flash, squeezing it tightly.

"Come now, Allison. Don't be afra—"

A loud thud in the living room caused me to flinch, and another quickly followed, making Paul frown and release me. We had no time to do anything else before I heard the front door break and smack against the wooden floor, then hurried footsteps into the house.

"Reno Police!" Liam shouted. "Allison—where are you?"

"We're in here!" I shouted back, immediately fleeing toward the open archway.

Liam met me there in seconds, his expression hard and his gun aimed in front of him. I said nothing and pointed to Paul, who still stood next to the basement door with a frown, but seemingly no fear. Their eyes locked before Liam turned his back to me, his gun aimed directly at Paul.

"Turn around and put your hands behind your back!"

Paul hesitated before he finally turned, though he kept his arms at his side. Liam closed the space between them and kept his gun pointed while he pulled a pair of cuffs from his pocket and cuffed Paul with one hand.

• • • • • •

Paul sat on the kitchen floor with his back against the wall while we waited an hour for the nearest available police to show up to the extremely remote town. During this time, Liam interrogated him further about Dana Carter and Becky Johnson, but Paul kept his gaze low and gave short answers.

I watched in silence most of the time, trying to reconcile how Paul actually acted compared to how I had imagined him. For an evil genius that could easily be very expressive, cruel and calculated, his general detachedness and now child-like disappointment threw me off. But ultimately, he *was* a killer and kidnapper regardless, even if that wasn't his true end goal.

When a police car with two officers arrived, Liam escorted Paul outside, and promptly contained him inside the secured backseat compartment. Liam then told the officers about our operation, and afterward, they headed inside the house.

"They're going to search the whole place, right?" I asked Liam while we stood near the police car. "I heard a door close upstairs when I was talking to Paul, so there might be someone else hiding in there."

Liam's eyes widened.

"What? Are you serious?"

"Yes, but honestly, I'm not sure. I never heard anything else, but Paul did go upstairs before we went into the kitchen."

Liam sighed and nodded.

"Yeah, they're going to search the place and collect any evidence. Are you alright?"

His hands gently rested on my shoulders, and I smiled as my gaze settled into his, which had a delightful mix of concern and affection.

"There were a few scary moments, but I'm alright. Thank you so much for this, Liam. You're a hero."

The corner of his mouth turned up as he pinched my chin lightly between his thumb and index finger.

"I'm not the only one. I'll be right back—I'm going to get the transmitter and turn it in."

I nodded before Liam left, and a minute later, I saw the two other police officers walk out of the house. When they neared me, I tucked away a loose strand of hair and noticed a large plastic baggy in the hand of the taller officer.

"What do you think of the black machine?" I asked both of them. "Paul uses it to lethally dose people with radiation, and I know someone who has examined it professionally.

She can testify that it was made for unethical and illegal purposes."

"Hmm, what machine?" the officer with the baggy asked.

I blinked, furrowing my eyebrows.

"The big black one in the basement. Didn't you search the house?"

"We did," the other officer replied. "But it was mostly empty, and there certainly wasn't a machine like that in the basement. What we found were these syringes lying on top of a shelf down there. We'll need to send them to the lab to know exactly what's in them, but I doubt it's anything good."

"Syringes?"

My thoughts froze as I felt unable to make sense of these new revelations. The mysterious black machine *had* to be in the basement, otherwise—why did Paul want to take me down there?

Unless...

Was he going to drug me? But why? What then?

The hair on the back of my neck rose as I then knew I hadn't been the only one playing a trick. My gaze slowly drifted to the backseat of the cop car, where I saw Paul's heavy gaze upon me through the barred window. His empty expression gave me a chill, and reminded me of a mannequin shell—as though the real Paul had fled his body now that he'd been arrested. But after a few seconds of locked gazes, Paul looked away.

"We also have a slight suspicion someone else may have been in the house recently."

My heart palpitated as I looked at the officer with the baggy and endured a fresh flood of horror.

"What? Why?"

"In one of the rooms upstairs, we found an open window with a fire escape ladder hanging down from it. It's in perfect condition, like it's never been used until today. The grass at the bottom is also freshly disturbed. When you were with him, was there any indication of another person being there?"

I nodded, my face overcome with shock.

"Y-yes. I heard a door close upstairs while we were in the living room, but nothing else."

"Alright, thank you. We'll gather that ladder and once Liam hands over the confession recording, we'll be on our way."

"Okay."

My stomach felt sick as I stared at the ground, feeling more like a fool in this situation than I ever thought possible. Much had been slithering beneath the surface of my encounter with Paul than I had reason to assume, and now, I just wanted to snap my fingers and immediately return home. Draw the curtains and wrap myself in a blanket to escape into safety and familiarity for as long as I could.

I took a deep breath.

There's nothing to worry about anymore...

Paul would go to prison now for his recorded confession and justice would be had soon, though sadly too late for his victims to enjoy. And as for the true whereabouts of the black machine... I could only hope the next hands it fell into would see it for what it was, and destroy it.

But at last, my insane mission was complete.

The end of the rabbit hole.

About the Author

Erika's first memory of her love for writing comes from elementary school, where she was given a small (but very exciting!) blank book to fill as an assignment. Some of her favorite pastimes are campfires, movie nights, and looking at dreamy coastal homes online.